For April

Book 1
Novella Couplet

Jillian Jacobs

Published by Green Moose Productions
Copyright 2017 by Jillian Jacobs

ISBN: 978-1-942313-14-4

DEDICATION

To Jeremy.

ACKNOWLEDGMENTS

To my beta-girls. Also thanks to Linda Carroll-Bradd. Best editor ever. Any mistakes are my own.

Other Books by Jillian Jacobs

The Elementals Series

Water's Threshold

Fire's Field

Air's Vision

The O-Line Series

Ember's Center

Rachel's Guard

Maude's Score

Clayton's Star

Kindle Worlds- **Infidelity World**

Insider

Novella Duet

For April

For Ryan – coming June 2017

CHAPTER 1

Ryan Cole ran a hand across his wrinkled Jiffy Oil shirt. Meeting a United States senator while sporting his day job's uniform—a gray shirt and plain black work-pants—wasn't exactly how he'd envisioned reuniting with the man, but apparently fate had other plans. Or maybe it was karma. Not that either had been particularly good to him, and he didn't expect that to change anytime soon.

Walking to this teashop from his apartment already had him sweating. Long sleeves during a humid day in Central Indiana wasn't a smart move, but between his day job, his night job as a bartender, and online law classes, he had zero time for pain-in-the-ass chores like ironing. Nor did he have time for appointments with politicians. Heaving a sigh, he pulled on the shop's door handle, took the step up, and blinked, allowing his eyes to adjust after being outside in the sun. He caught a glimpse of blond perfectly-trimmed hair by the front window and headed in that direction.

"Good morning, Mr. Cole." Senator Paul David waved him over.

A bright red tie topped his navy blue suit. Typical. Dude even had the little American flag pinned to his lapel. A handsome older man, his age likely upward of fifty-five, the stylish dark frames he wore highlighted his blue eyes.

"Sir." Ryan nodded and shook his hand before raking his fingers through the side of his shortly cropped dark blond hair. The top was longer and needed a trim. A fact he'd likely not care about if David weren't also a partner at one of the top law firms in the state—a law firm he'd give his left nut to work at. Taking online and local university classes, he'd completed his Bachelor's in political science, and he had scored in the top range on his LSAT. However, further schooling had become an issue due to lack of money, which added a harsh sense of never-gonna-happen to his dreams of becoming an attorney.

"Let's sit." Senator David pointed toward a flowery upholstered chair.

The area at the front of the teashop was like some kind of tea-drinking-cocoon. His oil-stained attire in no way matched the colorful couch David settled onto. Flowers and tea—he'd never felt more out of place.

"Can I get you something to drink?"

Ryan merely raised a brow then shook his head. Unless the beverage was black wake-up-the-dead coffee he had no interest.

"No? Fine, then I'll get right to the purpose of this meeting." David leaned forward with his elbows on his knees, dangling his to-go cup between his legs. "First of all, I want to thank you for what you did for me."

"Sir, I—"

"No, no." The senator lifted his hand, palm out. "I made a grave mistake, and you helped me rather than using my misfortune to make a profit. I appreciate that more than you'll ever know. In my position, I don't trust anyone, but...something about you makes me believe I can put a little faith in you."

Around a month ago, Ryan left a "friend's" apartment late one night and noticed a Cadillac resting sideways in a ditch with smoke pouring from the engine. The senator was drunk and injured, but cognizant enough to know that the police and the media couldn't discover his incident. Aware of the need for discretion, Ryan called a friend who owned a tow-truck company and took the senator to a nurse he'd dated.

Honestly, he'd love some gratitude in the form of this influential man offering him a job...but his cynical nature stood up and said, Hold on there, cowboy. "Why would you have faith in me, Senator David?" Ryan shook his head. "You don't even know me."

David shrugged. "I've found it's what people do when no one is watching that counts." He glanced around the shop.

What he was looking for Ryan couldn't say, as the only other inhabitants were the guy behind the counter and a big guy, maybe-early twenties, dressed in a finely-cut gray suit that didn't match his cauliflower-ears or scarred nose.

While pretty fit himself at six-two and one-ninety, Ryan would rather not wrestle with Mr. I-can-lift-an-elephant-with-my-pinky, leaning against the counter.

The Senator twisted in his seat and faced the man. "Dewey, leave us a moment."

Dewey glanced at Ryan then nodded and stepped outside.

The senator rubbed his hands up and down his thighs. "I'll begin." He cleared his throat and took a drink from his to-go cup before meeting Ryan's gaze. "You may or may not be aware, but I have a daughter. I've struggled over the best way to proceed with her, but I-I...you see, ever since I met you, I've had this crazy idea stirring in my mind. So bear with me, because I believe what I want will become clear after you hear April's story."

"April is your daughter?"

"Yes. I've raised her as well as I can since her mother...passed." He cleared his throat again. "Are you sure you don't need anything?"

"No." Not unless they had a nice bottle of whisky hidden behind all those tea canisters. And was it hot in here? It seemed hot in here. He tugged on his collar. Why should he care about some spoiled politicians daughter? Yet, curiosity kept him in his seat. "Go on."

"My wife, Anna, was born and bred to be a senator's wife. Her family came from the East Coast. Old money and old connections. We met while I attended Harvard. Anna was a few years older, but that didn't matter. We aligned perfectly. She had this poise and grace you don't see much nowadays. A true lady. Strong-willed and intelligent. The perfect wife for a man with my political aspirations. As expected of such women, she volunteered with various national charities and traveled to third-world countries."

Ryan nodded, having a suspicion this story did not end well, especially when the man used past tense words like *had*.

"Once she could walk, April frequently accompanied Anna. Since we'd campaigned as a family, my wife was well known. Because of her popularity, when she went to Sierra Leone for the second time, she and April were abducted and held for ransom."

"I'm sorry." Ryan winced, wishing he actually had a drink now. Plus, saying sorry never changed anything. *Sorry, you have to live with your Mom's abusive boyfriends, Ryan. Sorry, there's nothing to eat. Sorry, you have to live in a roach-infested apartment.* Empty words, but sorry was all he could think to say. "While I commend your wife for her efforts, I don't know that I'd ever travel to such places like Africa. Hell, I've barely been out of Indiana, so if I had a chance to escape, it'd be all pleasure." All pleasure? *What the hell am I talking about? The guy is wrenching open his heart, and I'm talking about taking pleasure trips.* God, he was such an idiot.

"I understand and agree. I should have been more aware of the dangers surrounding Anna's travel choices." David sighed and leaned back in his seat. "I don't know how familiar you are with militant groups, but they have no moral compass. And...my wife and April were treated as prisoners in every sense of the word...exposed to many horrors." He closed his eyes for a moment then took a deep breath. "When my wife finally returned home, she was a completely different person, especially due to some…scarring on her face. April has never spoken of her time there. She was just a little girl…seven years old."

The senator stared out the window, which was covered with the shop's logo—a steaming tea cup. A warm, welcoming image so at odds with cold, dark story being relayed inside.

"Those were very difficult times for our family. Both April and Anna became sullen and withdrawn." He stood and paced in the small space between the couch and the coffee table—or in this instance, tea table.

Ryan certainly understood dark times and losing a mother. He rubbed his temples. *Sweet baby Jesus, what am I doing here?* Opening up about the past wasn't something he'd ever do, so what did this guy want? Would it be rude to pull out his phone and check the time, because Jesus, he needed to get to work.

"You might find this a bit ironic, Mr. Cole."

Ryan arched a brow, sure this next admission would be a doozy.

"Approximately a year after Anna returned, she took April for a car ride." The senator sucked in a breath. "She deliberately crashed the vehicle into a tree and didn't survive. April, however, did." He tucked both hands in his front pockets and rocked back on his heels. "Anna's suicide mission never made it to the press. Which will continue to be the case."

Damn. This story just kept getting worse, and by the way the Senator was staring at him, he was expected to respond. "Right. Of course I won't say anything. I'm sorry for your loss, but I'm still not seeing what this has to do with me." Ryan fingered his phone, considering texting his boss for real. This conversation was obviously going to last a bit longer.

"I don't know what to do about April." David threw up both hands. "After the accident, she was…well, basically, we had to institutionalize her for a few years. But then she requested to come home, and since that time she has done well."

Institutionalized? He'd been jacked up as a kid, but not that much. As memories of his less-than-pleasant childhood threatened to break past his internal barriers, he heaved in a deep breath. The fruity-floral tea aromas fired up his nose and added to a brewing headache. Plus, the owner really needed to turn up the air conditioning. Or maybe he just needed to calm his shit. "Again, I think you called me here for a reason, and I'm still not seeing it."

"You're a very social guy." The senator sank onto the couch. "Friendly, reliable. Plus, as a bartender, I imagine you meet and talk with all kinds of people. I've researched your background, and you and April, well to be blunt, neither of you have had the best go of life. I'm hoping the tragedies in your past will help in your understanding of my daughter."

Clarity started to sink in. This guy thought to set up some kind of playdate where he and this April chick sat around and cried about the past. *Fuck that.* Straightening, Ryan shook his head. "You want me to understand your daughter? Sorry, but how's that supposed to work? I'm not a psychologist. And I'm not as friendly as you think." Plus, no way in hell would he ever discuss his childhood with anyone. Ever.

"I understand your reticence." David's already blindingly white teeth sparkled even more with the light shining in from the window. "However, April has made more frequent forays out and about, just here locally. We live in a townhouse on Main Street." The senator tapped his cup against his palm. "Yet, your assessment is correct, I'd like you to be where she is. I've talked to the owner of this shop, Mr. Jones. He's willing to take you on, and I'll make up the difference between what he pays you and what you would've made at the oil-change establishment."

"Wait. Back up a second…you want me to work *here*." Ryan huffed out a laugh as he imagined holding a dainty teacup in his hand and lifting his pinky as he took a sip. "I don't know anything about tea."

"That's irrelevant, because you know people, and you can learn the rest quickly." David shifted forward in his seat. "I see something in you...a hunger. A vision of myself at your age. This can work."

"You're mistaken if you think who I am aligns with any vision you have, or even *had*, of yourself." Ryan was familiar with those high-dollar apartments on Main Street. A couple of his buddies worked construction on those jobs. No way did his twenty-five year old self ever align with who the Senator was at that same age. Nope. Not even close. He'd come from the complete other side of the tracks. Although...he did hunger for more, that was true. "Listen, you don't *really* know me. I'm not the guy for this...scheme, or whatever it is. Not only that, how the hell would I know where April is?"

"She comes here"—the Senator waved a hand around the shop—"every Tuesday and Thursday at ten a.m. My daughter likes her schedules. Everything neat and orderly."

"I'm not neat or orderly." Ryan folded up the right sleeve of his shirt.

"Exactly."

That tone suggested a very big *gotcha*. "No, not *exactly*, not even close. Look at me." He waved a hand over his arm's tattoos, and the piercings in his ears and left eyebrow. "I'm not the kind of guy you bring home to meet the parents, especially when one of the parents is a United States senator."

David's gaze swept up and down his tattoos. "If you removed the earrings, I'd say you're a decent-enough looking kid. And I'm not asking you to marry her, just help her socialize." The senator rubbed his clean-shaven chin. "I've coddled her too much. She's lost so many years, and I want her to experience more in life. Right now, she's wasting away. She needs someone who can give her a shove in the right direction. Show her friendship and help her socialize with those her own age."

A shove? Friendship? What is this guy talking about? Ryan wasn't the guy to save some princess from an ivory tower. As a matter of fact, the idea churned his stomach. "Why don't *you* talk to her? Or have your big gorilla, Dewey give her a shove?"

"I tried." The senator heaved a sigh. "I don't understand her. I love her, but I've never been able to reach her in any significant way. And that is my fault. I own that responsibility. I've not spent as much time with her as I should, and in the time I do spend, well...we don't always see eye-to-eye."

"Maybe she needs tough love, and I'm not sure you want *me* doing the shoving." Family drama wasn't his thing. He'd been there, done that. Wasn't keen on doing it again.

David slouched in his seat, rubbing a hand against his temple. "I'm her father, not her friend. She needs an outside connection. Someone who can show her what people her age do. I have no idea about those sorts of things."

"Well, my friends sure as hell don't sit around sipping tea." Ryan snorted. "Can't you speak to a therapist, or whoever? You may think April and I have a lot in common, but based on that story, I'm gonna say no. She got out of her hell, I lived in mine until I was thirteen."

"Are there different degrees of hell?" The senator arched a brow.

"In my opinion, yeah."

"I didn't live in your hell, nor did I live in April's, so I can't say."

Ryan considered all the times he'd prayed for someone to come along and ransom him out of his hell. Spending time in an institution with warm food and a warm bed seemed like a better way to go than some of the shabby shitholes he'd been forced to endure. Still, the senator was right, this chick had likely seen hell while captured. Not only that, she'd lost her mom. That didn't mean they had anything in common—well, besides losing their mothers, and yeah, they'd both had horrible childhoods. *Damn it!* He didn't do handholding, hugging, or any of that pansy-assed shit. "I'm sorry for your daughter's...situation, but I'm not helping some teen get over her childhood traumas. I got enough of my own."

"She's not a teen, she's twenty."

"Yeah, well, still." Ryan stood and pulled his buzzing phone from his pocket. "My boss is texting me. I need to head out."

"Sit back down, please. You haven't heard my offer."

"Yeah I kind of did, and I don't think I can help. Sorry." He glanced at his phone and the colorful text from his boss at the oil and lube shop, Jason.

"Sit, Mr. Cole. I believe I can change your mind."

After reminding himself the senator was an influential lawyer, which aligned with his future plans, Ryan pecked out a note to Jason, basically telling him he'd be there when he got there. "I got like ten minutes then I really gotta go."

"Very well." David pointed a hand toward the chair.

Ryan sat though still unsure why he hadn't left long before now.

"Please understand, I'm not just doing this for my daughter. I'm doing this for you, as well."

Here comes the political speech.

"You helped me, so let me return the favor."

Ryan opened his mouth to speak.

The senator lifted a hand. "All I ask is that you make a concerted effort to befriend April this summer, and if you do this for me...I'll pay for the next four years of your education."

Stunned, Ryan sat silent for a moment. "What's the catch? What if *I* want to go to Harvard? Still plan on forking over the funds?"

"If you were listening earlier, you heard my wife came from old money and when she died that money came to me and to April. I do well enough from the law firm and my current position. You see, Ryan, I intend to go even farther someday. Do you understand?"

Ryan nodded, still caught up in dollar signs that could erase college debt, and not really considering what *farther* actually meant.

"As I move forward in my political career, my past will be ripped apart. April is not strong enough to endure any sort of invasion of her privacy, nor will I allow such a thing. But, at some point, I need her to overcome her past and stand strong. She is Anna Roberts's daughter, and she was meant for more than cowering in her room. I need your assistance, and I will repay you the debt I owe."

Damn, the guy really gives an impassioned speech. "What you're asking of me…it's a heavy task."

"I will not lie and say helping April won't be challenging. She's very set in her ways and extremely guarded."

Ryan considered the assignment. He'd always been a charmer. After wheedling his way out of trouble for twenty-five years, he'd become an expert at finding just the right angle to get what he wanted. This skill was part of why he'd make a fantastic lawyer. This was one of those moments in life when he had to leap and say, fuck the consequences. "Fine." He shrugged. "I'll help her out."

"Great." A huge grin split the Senator's face. He rounded the tea table and shook Ryan's hand. "I'll have my assistant type up the particulars. I'm sure I don't have to remind you this is strictly confidential." He tightened his grip. "I can help you, or I can destroy you."

Eyes wide, Ryan chuckled. "Nice. We've moved on to threats already, and you don't even know me. Most people wait at least two weeks before they want to ruin me."

"This is a very serious undertaking." David braced a hand on his shoulder. "Never thought you'd be anyone's white knight, huh?"

"Your princess will soon learn, I'm no hero." Ryan shook his head, unable to believe he was actually agreeing to this madness. "I'll help your daughter, but just so you know, after spending the summer with me, she might return to the institution."

"You think you're being funny, but after you meet her, I predict your whole life will change." The senator winked.

And with that simple movement a chill traveled down Ryan's spine, as if fate were walking with its bare, icy feet down his back. But after saying his goodbyes, he stepped outside, and the promise of a paid-for Ivy League education warmed his bones.

CHAPTER 2

After spending the morning talking tea with the shop's owner, Mr. Jones, Ryan adjusted the tin canisters again then wiped the countertop for the third time in the past fifteen minutes. Unclear where these nerves were coming from, he frowned. For years, he'd served people over a bar. This shouldn't be any different, but for some reason waiting for this girl had him on edge. The senator had set him up to work on days when April frequented the teashop, which meant his "real" summer job would begin soon.

Brewing tea was actually quite simple: scoop out a couple teaspoons, heat the water to a certain temperature, and then let the tea leaves steep. Much easier than some of the cocktails he shook and stirred at Galaxy on Friday and Saturday nights.

When Dewey, aka big dude, had dropped off the befriend-April-for-paid-college contracts yesterday, he'd shown Ryan a few pictures of the woman on his phone. The images weren't up close, but from what he could tell, she *was* quite a beauty. Still, how would he handle her antisocial behavior? This whole idea was one big mistake, but a full education was on the line, so he'd see this through.

Leaning against the counter, Ryan shot to attention when the woman from the photos stepped through the door. Her flawless face damn near struck him blind. Wavy, just past the shoulders, blonde hair, light blue eyes, and not a drop of makeup on her face—the pictures hadn't done her justice. Naturally beautiful and tall, like a fashion model all fresh-faced before she prepared for a photo shoot where they sexed her up.

He'd known his fair share of gorgeous women, but this was his every fantasy in one package. He shifted behind the counter, trying to readjust his slight erection, which was absolutely inappropriate but completely out of his control. He'd never believed in love at first sight, but April David just might be capable of changing his mind.

She stopped just inside the door and, with a tilt of her head, stared at him while squeezing her hands together at her waist. Her clothes reminded him of a school uniform: tan pants and a navy-blue polo shirt. They matched, as he'd worn his best jeans and a long sleeve navy Henley, even though it was hot as shit outside. The shirt covered the tattoos on his arms, so he wouldn't look like a punk. "Good morning, beautiful. What can I get you?"

Her head slanted a little more to the left yet she remained by the door for a moment before inching further into the room and peering toward the back storage area.

"Jones is running some errands. I'm Ryan, by the way." He smiled. "Don't be shy. Come here."

April blinked then met his gaze. Her eyes were like some doe caught in the light beam of a speeding freight train.

He caught a glimpse of a hearing device in her left ear through a small part in that shiny blonde hair. What the hell was that? David hadn't mentioned she was deaf. Did he need to sign or something? Speak louder?

She took a small step toward the counter, and then glanced over her shoulder at the exit.

No. No. Don't bolt. Not with a full ride to Harvard-town on the line. "Usually when someone introduces themselves, the other person reciprocates."

Her gaze shot from the door to him.

Ah, so she could hear him.

Brow furrowed, she bit her bottom lip and took the final steps to the counter. "Earl Grey."

He flashed a cocky grin. "Your name is Earl Grey?"

"No. My name is April."

Her pale cheeks turned a slight pink, and her voice boomed through the small tearoom. A nice voice, but loud. Perhaps she was nervous, or maybe this was her natural tone due to her hearing deficiency.

"Earl Grey it is, and you don't have to speak so loud." He winked.

She gasped then turned on her heel to leave.

Highlighting the woman's deficiencies? Great way to make friends, dumb ass. "Hey, wait." Ryan hopped over the counter and caught her right as she grabbed the door handle. He covered her hand.

She yanked away. "Don't touch me."

"Sorry, sorry." He dropped his hand to the side. "Listen, I was just teasing. Come back, and I'll brew your tea. I promise I won't say another word, all right?"

Still rubbing the place where he'd touched her, she shook her head.

"Please, I don't want to lose this job. I've got a hungry mouth to feed...my own." He flashed another smile, the one his friend, Lori, called his sure-to-melt-their-panties grin.

In the same loud voice, she answered, "Earl Grey."

He nodded then mimed zipping his lips closed and throwing away the key.

True to his word, he brewed her tea and didn't say another word.

She grabbed her cup off the counter and hightailed it out of the shop like caffeine monsters would sprout from his ears.

Smooth, Cole. Real smooth.

# # #

"How was your visit with April today?"

Ryan held his cell up to his ear, considering the best way to answer the senator's question. Leaning against his kitchen counter, he studied the worn rug he'd tucked under the cabinets. He'd have to get a new one soon. Domestic décor wasn't his thing, but cleanliness was. After living in shitholes his entire childhood, he wasn't about to continue that practice. Although, he did have one weakness—laundry.

"Where the hell have you been keeping her?" The more he'd thought about April—her schoolgirl costume, her fear, her odd voice—the angrier he'd become. Though, how she evoked such a strong emotion, he was still working out. Caring about people never got him anything but pain and disappointment, so why? He shook his head. He knew why. She was trapped, just like his mother had been...just like he'd been. He couldn't save his mother, but maybe he could save April. Though he wasn't sure a surly cynic like him was the right man to bring hope and rainbow-colored happiness to some spoiled rich kid. Why couldn't the senator, with all his money, pay for a professional to help his daughter? "I'm not so sure about this plan. She's like a frightened kitten."

"She *is* frightened, yes," David answered in a smarmy "no-duh" tone. "So now you understand my dilemma?"

"I understand she's an innocent wrapped in a siren's body."

"You aren't to engage her body, just her mind. She may seem innocent, but she's very intelligent, just not socially adept."

That was the understatement of the year. "I believe you forgot to mention something very critical. Is she deaf?"

"Partially."

"Okay...and how'd that happen?" Nice that Sir Senator added on this tidbit after the contracts were signed. What else was he leaving out?

"When she was...kept, the men...they injured both sides of

her head. The doctors feel that this trauma was…ah…done repeatedly. They believe she was hit with the butt of a rifle."

Fucking hell. Ryan rubbed his ear. "They damaged her ear enough that she's deaf?"

"Yes. Almost fully on the right and some hearing loss on the left."

"Did anything else happen? Like did the men, you know?" Ryan hesitated…sure rape was an inappropriate topic with a senator…or anyone.

"No, but her therapist, Dr. Ashburn believes she saw things." The senator sniffed.

"Damn." Ryan winced. Maybe this April girl *was* tough. And if she had a therapist, what the hell was the point of his involvement?

"Did she speak to you?"

"Barely."

"Well, keep at it. Like I said, we'll give this project the summer."

Summer. Three months. He could do this. *Eye on the prize, Cole.* "No problem, boss."

Ryan heard a sigh right as the senator hung up. The guy really didn't know what kind of man he was working with. Or, maybe he did. David had said he'd checked into his background. So the senator likely knew about Ryan's mother and the merry-go-round of men in and out of their lives. He likely knew one of those men had finally killed her. But how much more did Senator David know?

Ryan's goal to become a lawyer began, because guys like the one who had killed his mother got off on technicalities or by pleading insanity. The man who'd killed his mother wasn't insane, just stone cold evil, as with most of the losers she'd brought home.

She'd had Ryan at fifteen. Her parents were equally messed up, so she'd never had a chance. An addict who worked to feed her habit, she'd died when he was thirteen. After that, he shifted between a few foster homes.

Those nice folks in his foster homes couldn't change his downward trajectory, but the not-guilty verdict in his mother's case had halted that plunge with jarring impact. The unfairness of everything finally hit home, creating a burning need to seek justice.

His final foster dad had said, "Do something about it." Not profound, but for a kid with no direction, those few words fueled the spark inside.

At the library, he'd read every law book and true crime story he could find, fascinated by cases similar to his mom's. During his senior year, his foster mother helped him apply to a local college, and he'd gone for four years.

But after he'd started tending bar at Galaxy—the hottest dance club in town—he'd become distracted by the women, booze, and drugs flowing freely through the place. This last year, he'd refocused on his mental and physical health. And a few months after that decision, he'd pulled the senator from the ditch.

He'd been given a second chance to fulfill his dream. Perhaps he'd needed that short break to get everything out of his system. To live freely without fear for his mother's life and his own. He was in control now, though he'd have to maintain a look-but-don't-touch policy where April was concerned.

Stomach growling, he opened his fridge and pulled out the makings for a sandwich. He needed fuel to power through all these mind-bending thoughts.

Did he have the patience to deal with some woman who'd been pampered by daddy? Why couldn't she just move on? Others had. He had. Okay, so maybe he did have a hard time trusting people. Maybe he'd never given his heart to another. And, perhaps he could be abrasive at times. He'd admit to a lot of unresolved anger. However, he'd chosen to live every day. Worked hard. Played hard. Fucked hard. How did a guy like him who pushed boundaries relate to a woman who could barely leave her house?

He'd push her. That's what he'd do. He'd make her stand at an edge and give her the shove the senator had asked for. He wouldn't watch another woman waste away. Not this time.

CHAPTER 3

After spending the morning "wafting aromas" of white, green, oolong, and rooibos tealeaves through his nose, Ryan winced as the shop's door bells chimed. So many flavors shooting through his nostrils had his temples throbbing.

Last night, he'd resolved how to handle April. Full-bore. No-nonsense. They had little time, and she'd been spoiled long enough. He had this chance, and he'd kick start Ms. April's transformation starting today.

"Good morning, April. How are you?" He placed one hand on the check-out counter and flashed a grin.

"I would like an Earl Grey to go, please." Cheeks pink and hands rubbing together overtime in front of her waist, she didn't even meet his gaze as she placed her order.

"Nah. Nope." Shaking his head, Ryan settled back against the prep station's worktop and folded both arms across his chest. "You see, April, when someone says good morning and how are you, you say, I'm well, or however you're feeling, and then you ask, how are you? Kind of rude, otherwise."

"I just want my tea." She sniffed, lifting her chin to meet his gaze with a bit of a narrow-wrinkle alongside those blue eyes.

Interesting. How much more spark was buried beneath that enticing blue? "First, I can hear you, so tone it down. The second thing, be kind to those of us making minimum wage."

"That is not funny." She mumbled so softly he barely heard her.

"What's not funny?"

"Making fun of how I talk." Her voice turned louder now. "I can't help it."

"Why not?"

Meeting his gaze, she pointed at her ears. "I'm nervous, plus I'm basically deaf in my right ear, and my left ear is damaged, as well."

"Oh, well then." He turned to fix her tea. "Guess that means I'll treat you differently than everyone else. Guess I won't point out that you speak loudly, which I think has more to do with your shyness than your ears."

"I have no idea what you're talking about, and to be honest, *Sir*. I don't think you do either."

He held back a grin at her haughty little "sir." "You want me to treat you the same as everyone else, don't you?" He glanced over his shoulder, arching a brow.

"I come here for tea, not conversation or to be treated rudely and have my imperfections pointed out. And why do you say I'm shy? Perhaps I don't feel comfortable speaking to strangers."

Releasing a sigh, he shrugged. "Five minutes to steep."

"Thank you."

He held a hand by his ear. "What'd you say?"

She narrowed her eyes quite obviously this time. "Talk about rude. You should be ashamed...and fired."

"Yeah, probably...but now we've got your blood pumping." He placed his hands on the countertop and leaned forward. "Your cheeks are rosy from anger not fear, and those blue eyes have a spark, like a fluffy yellow kitten who's learning to pounce."

She didn't answer just rubbed her hands together again and stared everywhere but at him. Though, she was likely cursing him mentally.

Once the timer went off, he capped her tea with a to-go lid. They exchanged money without another word, which wasn't in line with his plans, so he reached across the counter and tipped up her chin. "April, look at me."

She flinched and pulled away. "I asked you not to touch me. I'm sure Mr. Jones wouldn't want you manhandling the customers."

"Again, you're probably right," Ryan nodded and tucked his hand back at his side. Now that she was closer, he detected something floral, like roses. The scent suited her: delicate, blooming, and beautiful. "I tend to say what's on my mind. Sorry if I offended you, but you seem so straight-laced. I can't help but want to shake you up a little."

She pursed her lips. "Sometimes saying everything that's on your mind isn't wise or kind. Nor is touching someone without their permission."

He smiled. From kitten to tiger. Well, well…this was progress. "Maybe that's true, but speaking my mind is honest and keeps things real. Are you real, April?"

She held her cup high by her chest. "I don't—"

The jangle of the door interrupted her. A group of four elderly ladies sauntered in, oohing and aahing over the place.

Great. He hoped they didn't ask for anything too complicated. He winked at April. "We'll talk next time. I'll try to find some manners."

"Please do." She nodded and turned to leave. At the door, she stopped, glanced over her shoulder and started to speak. But then, shook her head and left

# # #

Two weeks into Project Befriend April, and Ryan had made little progress. When she came to the teashop, she didn't stay and read like her father had indicated. So Ryan spent that time catching up on his own reading, prepping for more classes in the fall. He'd already applied to area colleges, but on a whim, he sent applications to East Coast schools, as well. Why not? He had nothing to lose, except everything, and the way things were going with April didn't bode well for his collegiate future. Her father called him frequently, not at all pleased with his strides toward making April a social butterfly.

Tuesday, though, she'd finally stayed and read at her table. So Ryan left her alone, pretending to fuss behind the counter for two hours. Everything in him wanted to sit down and dig into that beautiful head, but he let her be. He wasn't the type of guy to sit back and wait. He jumped in, head first, balls to the wall. This hesitant, polite side of himself April had drawn forth was grating on his nerves.

Today, he'd delivered her tea with minimal banter and breathed a sigh of relief when she stayed again. She didn't sit on the couches but at one of the little tables with rickety wooden chairs that folded up.

He called Jones from the back to man the counter and maneuvered closer to his prey. "What are you reading?" He glanced over April's shoulder. "Last time, you were over here for hours on that thing."

She stilled then placed her device on the table. "I-I like true crime stories."

"Yeah? Me, too." Making himself comfortable in the chair across from her, he shoved his fingers through his hair, and mentally took note he still needed a trim. "As a matter of fact, I'm studying to be a lawyer."

"Really?" She glanced at the full sleeve of tattoos on his arm.

That look usually carried a lot of preconceived notions, which normally irritated him, but he was edgy enough already, so he let it drop. He'd given up hiding his tattoos because she was already a frightened kitten around him, wasn't like a few drawings on his skin mattered at this point. "You got any ink?"

She tilted her head. "No, I didn't bring a pen. I'm sorry."

He chuckled. "No. Ink." He pointed to his arm. "Do you have any tattoos?"

"No." Her eyes widened, and she shook her head.

Her blonde hair danced in waves around her shoulders. So thick and lush with that hint of roses still evident even with all the tea leaf aromas floating through the room. What would it feel like slipping between his fingers?

She isn't for you, Cole. Tone it down.

"If you could get a tattoo, what would it be?"

"Oh, I wouldn't." She bit her bottom lip and ran a finger along the edge of her e-reader. Her fingers were long and pale. No rings, no scars, just creamy flesh leading to blunt natural-colored nails. What would those smooth hands feel like on his skin? *And stop! Distracted much?*

If he could get her to pick a type of tattoo, maybe he'd be able to read her a little better. Ink said a lot about a person. "Right, I get that you wouldn't actually ever get one, but work with me here?" He leaned back in his chair, momentarily worried the rickety thing would fracture under his weight. "Say, you went crazy one day and decided to get a tattoo. Would you get a panda? No, a kitten?" He laughed.

April's lips lifted, the first true smile she'd ever shared, but then she sighed and stared out the window for a moment. "I would get a bird."

He studied the lines of her jaw and the device in her ear as she gazed out the window, as if waiting for a bird to fly by. "What kind?"

"Any, really." She shrugged then met his gaze.

"Why a bird?"

She cleared her throat and placed those beautiful fingers against the side of her neck. "Because birds can fly away."

This statement was given in a quiet tone, as if she shared a secret. Again, that primal instinct to protect roared to life, rising until it fired across the tip of his heart. He mentally shook his head. Out of all the women he'd ever met, this was the one to stir his heart? The princess and the peon. Never gonna happen. Still, he'd take this moment and cherish the understanding between two people who'd dared to dream of flying far, far away. "Where would you go?"

"Go?" The light from the picture window glinted off her sad blue eyes as her brow furrowed. "I don't want to leave. I meant if I was trapped somewhere, then as a bird, I could escape."

"I see. You know, the type of tattoo you choose reveals a lot about who you are." He flicked a finger at her Kindle. "True crime books and a wish to escape…hmm, you just became more interesting." A statement that with each passing day became more and more true. He wanted to crawl inside her mind and dig out everything. Wanted to grip her thick blonde hair, bend her back, and kiss her. He may have startled her when she'd come into the teashop, unaware of the changes to come, but he was the one shaken. And he hated feeling unsettled and unsure. He'd thought he had moved past his childhood demons but obviously they still lurked in deep, dark corners of his soul. By helping her maybe he'd free himself, too. Yet, did he want to change? Wasn't he happy with his current state of being? Obviously not, because he'd agreed to this ridiculous scheme in order to change his future, and maybe he should consider what actually leaving this town would mean? Had he been stalling because he'd been afraid to move forward? *Hell.* He shook his head. Now was not the time for self-reflection.

"I don't know why I said that." April fiddled with the handle of her teacup. "About the bird…and escaping. I don't know where I'd go."

"We're friends and friends share those kinds of things." Now *he* didn't know why he'd said *that*.

Her head shot up, and she blinked. "Really?"

Her lovely features were filled with surprise and, maybe, a hint of hope. "Of course." The senator was right. He and April *were* a lot alike. Ryan had covered his body in tattoos representing his pain, but she'd internalized hers. What if she released everything she felt? What horrors would be written upon her body?

Suddenly, none of those musings mattered because she smiled, a wide grin lighting her whole face and sparkling in her eyes. Hell, if he'd known "friend" was the magic word, he'd have used it weeks ago. "Maybe someday we'll get you that tattoo, and you'll look at it and remember me and know you *are* free to fly."

She inhaled deeply then fluffed up her hair by her ear. A self-conscious habit he'd noted she did frequently, along with worrying her hands together. "I'm not sure a tattoo can do all that." She picked up her E-reader then put it back down and cleared her throat. "Do…um, do you like tea, Ryan?"

"Sometimes." He recognized her change of subject and allowed it before he revealed a piece of himself he never shared with anyone. "Some of the teas in this place seem palatable enough. The black teas, anyway." He nodded toward her cup. "Why do you always get the same thing?"

"You really want to know?" She met his gaze.

Those bright blue eyes, so different from his own muddy brown, seemed less wary now. "Sure." Though he remained unsure how many more secrets he could handle today. If she told him another story about wanting to escape, he might have to hang up his male card and buy a box of fucking tissues.

"My mom drank Earl Grey, and…I-I don't know…I feel closer to her when I smell it. When I drink it." A tear slipped down her cheek. "She'd fix it for me sometimes with an orange slice on top." She smiled again, but this time it didn't reach her eyes.

Well hell, sign him up for Kleenex delivery. "Is your mom dead, then?" Of course, he knew the answer, but she didn't know he knew. And wasn't that a tangled mess?

"I don't like to talk about it."

Since they were sharing, he decided to take the plunge, although he didn't like to talk about his past, either. "My mom's dead, too. Actually, she's the reason I'm going into law."

"Me, too. I mean, I'm studying law, too, but not because of my mom. My father is a lawyer, and I hope to make him proud someday." Tilting her head again, she gazed at him as if she'd never really seen him before.

He understood he was easy to write off as a freak with an odd haircut, tattoos, and metal in his face, although he'd removed all that before starting this tea parlor gig. Still, the idea of such a man with dreams of respectable employment probably seemed far-fetched to a girl who dressed with military precision and had not one mark upon her perfect skin—at least, that he could see. "Tell me about the book you're reading."

And she did…for a whole hour.

He even got them more to drink and a snack, which she didn't eat or touch. He suggested she meet him at the library on Saturday and help him study. She'd taken a long moment to reply before finally agreeing.

Now that he'd delved a little deeper, he realized April was very intelligent and quite capable of carrying on a lengthy conversation about the law, so why was she wasting her life hiding? Hadn't the therapist guy helped her move forward? And what was the point of developing this friendship if Ryan went away to school? Had the senator considered how April would feel if she lost a new friend? And could Ryan leave if he hadn't to some extent helped her? Saved her? The end game in this scheme just became more complicated, and he really hated complicated.

CHAPTER 4

Rubbing a hand over his bruised knuckles, Ryan angled back in the sturdy metal-and-plastic library chair. After sipping his black gas-station coffee, he glanced at the entrance again. The steaming liquid did nothing to ease his dark mood or lessen his tired soul. A bar fight last night, added to working not only as head bartender, but as cleaning crew both Thursday and Friday nights because an asshole called in sick, left his current disposition a fraction past lethal. Not to mention his confusion over how to handle April starring in his nightly naughty dreams. What kind of jerk lusted after an innocent woman? An asshole with a very kinky imagination, apparently.

He'd come to the library early, like some fawning jackass, in order to reserve a study room. Although he should have been studying, he spent more time rereading the same paragraph because he couldn't stop wondering if April would be brave enough to show up.

Her father said she rarely, if ever, strayed from her routine. If she met him here, he'd score high marks in this befriending assignment. Next would be getting her comfortable in other places, and with other people. Rubbing his tired eyes, he heaved a sigh.

This overwhelming, and slightly irrational, need to prepare

her for the world bore down on him daily. He often considered that perhaps she was better off hidden away. No one would appreciate her or understand her. No one except him. And that thought added fuel to his already cranky, sleep-deprived mind.

He glanced at the door. Again.

And there she was wearing tan pants and a navy blue polo, stepping through the doors, chin high, eyes darting through the room as if late for an afternoon high-society tea. Why she continued to dress like a snub-nosed private school student, he had no idea. Perhaps reworking her wardrobe should be part of his duties, which pissed him off. She had loads of money, didn't have to work for a living, didn't have to fall into a senator's plans, didn't have to clean fucking toilets a bunch of drunk people had shit, pissed, and puked all over, so what was her problem? Her life seemed pretty cake to him.

Some inner devil wanted to rough her up. He couldn't have her. Yet, she'd made him care about fixing her damaged parts. Standing, he whipped open the study-room door and called her over. Loudly. The librarian glared at him, but with the mood he was in he didn't give two-shits.

April jumped at his shout, and then she headed to the room. Once inside, she placed what looked like a brand new backpack on the table and dug out an equally new-looking notepad and pencil.

"What are you doing?" His irrational anger continued over her perfect little supplies.

"What do you mean?" She waved a hand at her bag. "I'm getting out my notebook."

In these tight quarters, her rosy scent came across strong enough to rush through his nostrils and shoot straight to his cock. He squirmed in his seat. "Do you even go to school?"

She sniffed. "Yes."

"Where?"

"I take…well I take online classes." Slowly lowering into her chair, she frowned as she pulled out her E-reader.

"What are you going to do with your degree? Besides make daddy proud?"

She gazed at him with furrowed brow, likely unsure of his biting tone. "I'm not sure. I'm working on…things." Cheeks turning a dark shade of pink, she smoothed her hands down her stupid tan pants.

"Why do you wear those clothes all the time?" Ryan waved a hand at her attire. "I mean you're how old, and you dress like you're in junior high?"

"I-I'm afraid I don't understand why my clothes matter."

"Because you look ridiculous. Where the hell do you even get them?"

She fingered the metal rings of her notebook over and over and over again. Her breathing turning ragged. "I…my clothes. I think Father has someone order them."

"Your *dad* buys your clothes?" Of course, he did.

Tossing her long blonde hair over her shoulder, she shrugged. "Who buys *your* clothes?" Her attempt at a snappy comeback was shattered by her wobbly voice.

"I do." Though aware he was being a royal-dick, April needed to understand women her age didn't dress like that and they sure as fuck didn't have daddy buying their clothes. Real people worked, jacked up credit card debt, and did their own laundry. He huffed out a laugh. She probably wouldn't even know how to separate a dark from a light. "What's your story, anyway? You wear odd clothes, come in for tea, and spend hours reading when most people work. Your dad buys your clothes. What's your damage, April?"

"I think I should go." She started to stand and flinched when he took her hand. "I'll ask you once again. Do not touch me."

"All right. Sorry. Now, sit down." He released her hand and waved her into back into the seat. "You want to be friends with someone, sometimes they ask harsh questions and tell you the truth about things you don't want to hear. I'm brutally honest. Always have been, always will be. You can't handle that, then we can't be friends." He glanced at the door and started to stand.

She gasped and gripped his arm—voluntarily.

"Wait…I-I don't want you to go." Her whole body shook. "I don't have any idea what I'm supposed to do, but I'm trying. Can't you see that?" She gazed up at him with tear-filled eyes. "I don't understand your tone today. Are you angry with me? If so, what have I done? I don't know how to be here. I don't know what's wrong with my clothes. I don't have any girlfriends to go shopping with. I was home schooled as a child, and I travelled with my mother, and then…and then…I got hurt, and my mom left me, and I…and I…please, don't go. Not yet." After she'd basically yelled loud enough for everyone in the library to hear he'd been complete ass, she laid her forehead against the table's edge and burst into tears.

"April, damn it…don't cry like that." Remorse firing through his system, he scooted his chair next to hers then wrapped her in his arms.

"D-don't t-touch me."

His heart and mind screamed against her restrictions, but he released her and fisted both hands at his sides. "I want to hold you, because I'm the one who made you cry. I'm not sorry for what I said. I don't understand *you,* either." They'd had a breakthrough and he meant to see it through, no matter how painful to her or to him. He tipped up her chin. "Look at me."

Body rigid, she hissed out a breath. "You are so cruel sometimes. Dr. Ashburn says I shouldn't speak to you anymore."

"I'm just what you need." Though he knew she'd cringed again, he wiped the tears from her cheeks. "Look at you, all snotty and covered in tears and yet, you're still the most beautiful thing I have ever seen." He ran a hand through his hair. "I'm sorry for making you cry. I had a rough couple nights at work, and you come in here all clean and perfectly cared for, and I don't know…our differences piss me off. Why do you have it so easy?"

She gaped at him, mouth slightly open. "You are mistaken if you believe my life is easy, Ryan. But, you're right. I need to make some changes, and I'm trying." She sniffed. "Can we be friends while I try?" Her voice softened. "I'll understand if I'm too much. I'm too much for myself, sometimes."

He should run for the fucking hills, because he was starting to see her as a person of interest and less as a job, and those thoughts would get him nowhere. She was too innocent for someone hard and empty like him. Yet, he wasn't as empty as he wished, not when he could see a whole lot of him, within her. "We're quite the pair, aren't we?"

"I hope so." She smiled and looked up at him from under wet lashes. "Maybe if you'd just said you had a bad day versus attacking me for things I cannot control, I wouldn't have had my outburst."

"You're right." He sighed. But *she* didn't have a clock ticking in the background like he did. They still had major strides to make and very little time to do so. "I don't know if it's in my nature to say I'm upset about things. That's not my style."

April pursed her lips. "But if you'd done so, I believe I wouldn't have become so upset or concerned I'd done something wrong. Dr. Ashburn thinks I should always reveal my feelings, or I—"

"No." Ryan held up a hand. "I don't want to know what he thinks. We both know you didn't do anything wrong. I guess…well, I mean…it seems you have some issues you need to work on, but maybe together we can bring some of that shit to the surface."

"Perhaps, but so far, I feel as if I'm the only one being pushed." Head down, she dug into her bag.

She hit the nail on the head with that comment. "I don't do heart opening reveals, April."

"Then how do you expect us to become friends?"

Geez, this woman was driving him mad. He ran a hand over his chin. "I don't know."

"Well…" She sniffed again. "Perhaps we'll begin by sharing our love of the law and leave some of the more personal topics for another time, yes?"

Oh, absolutely yes. His personal topics were a no go. Nope. Not happening. "Listen, again, I'm sorry, so yeah, let's just do what we came for." He studied her blotched cheeks and snotty nose. He'd done that. Maybe he wasn't the best guy to teach April how to become a friend. When had he ever let anyone inside? She was trying, and he wasn't. Not really. Forcing someone to blindly follow his own path wasn't building a friendship. If this were real, they'd need this whole friendship thing to develop more organically, but he didn't have that kind of time.

She wiped her nose. "Ryan?"

Her questioning tone indicated she'd been speaking to him yet he hadn't heard a word. "Stay here, I'll get some tissues."

"No," she practically shouted. "I have my own." She dug into her bag again and came out with hand wipes, sanitizer, and tissues. After she cleaned up, she leaned over and tapped his book. "What are you reading?"

The fact she moved on after his rude, and certainly uncalled-for, behavior made him respect her. She didn't dwell, simply took his words and actions at face value, determined, it seemed, to consider what he said. Likely, he would damage this poor woman worse than she already was. Still, his words needed to be said. She needed to understand who he was and where he was coming from. She needed to get better and, in order to do that, he would probably hurt her again and again. Maybe the real reason he pushed was because he wanted her to become *his* woman. Was he trying to mold her into his own ideal? Or was she already that woman? No, she simply called to a part of him that sought redemption. His mother hadn't had the resources to diverge off her broken road, but April did. If he could help her maybe he'd find some peace.

Peace or piece? Because he'd begun to believe that the only way he'd reach a peaceful end was with a piece of his heart molded together with a piece of April's, creating some semblance of a whole.

CHAPTER 5

Ryan had expected a visit from Dewey, but as June passed into July, he'd gone without the big guy banging down his door. They hadn't spoken even though Dewey frequently lingered outside the teashop. A bodyguard of some sort, it seemed. After meeting with April at the library, Ryan wasn't surprised to find the mammoth sitting on the steps outside his apartment, sunglasses drawn over his eyes and sweat trickling down his neck.

Ryan readjusted his grip on his overloaded grocery bags and dug his keys out of his jeans pocket. "I hope you haven't been sitting out here too long. It's humid as hell. Come on in for a beer." He might as well start the conversation on a congenial note.

Dewey nodded, stood, and then followed him inside.

Perhaps, the big guy had a day off, as he wasn't in his usual suit but wearing gym shorts and a faded T-shirt. "Senator David let you loose today?" Ryan stuffed his groceries in the fridge and grabbed two beers. "Make yourself comfortable." His apartment wasn't fit for any magazine spread, but he kept it clean and his furniture was only four years old. He hadn't splurged for a monster TV, because he never had time to watch. Anything he wanted to see, he just pulled up on his laptop. He handed Dewey a beer before sinking into the leather recliner.

Dewey still hadn't said a word, but he did settle his big frame onto the couch.

"I assume you're here to discuss April."

Dewey nodded then placed his beer on top of the wood coffee table. He scratched his head then stared down at the floor. "I understand what you and Mr. David are trying to accomplish, but neither of you are taking the long-term effects into consideration."

"And what is it we should be considering?" Ryan arched a brow and plopped his right ankle on his knee.

"Her suffering."

Those two words came out so pained, as if the big lug really did care. *Interesting.*

"Are you in love with her?"

Dewey shook his head. "I do love her as I would a sister, maybe even deeper, because I grew up watching over her. My uncle raised me, and since he is the senator's driver, we lived in the guesthouse back before Mr. David moved to town." He stood and paced behind the couch for a long moment. "You have no idea the pain April has endured. The change in her once she…when she came back."

Back from where? Likely the institution, but he wouldn't push that topic now. "I wouldn't do anything to hurt her."

"You may not *want* to hurt her, Cole, but you will. Her father is a good man, but he's busy with his career, and he doesn't know her like I do. I've seen a change in her lately. Yes, I'll admit your influence has been beneficial, but what happens when she learns the truth? What happens if you leave? She's become infatuated with you. Every word out of her mouth is Ryan this and Ryan that." He threw up both hands before locking them on his hips. "It's insanity."

Ryan definitely agreed with that. The more time he spent with April the more he believed she truly was a bird locked in a cage, but she was edging closer and closer to that open door. Would he still be here when she broke free? Or was Dewey right? Would she retreat once he left?

"You aren't the only one who worries about her." Ryan

straightened. "I'm trying to get her to a point where she can stand on her own."

Eyes downcast, Dewey shook his head. "See, that's where you're wrong. You cannot fix in three months who she's been since she came back from that...that place. You just can't." Releasing a low growl, he cursed and jabbed a finger at Ryan. "You don't really know her. You haven't seen her when she breaks. She has so many quirks and issues that you'll likely never know about. At any time, she could revert back to...to that emptiness, her blank stare." The mammoth actually shivered. "You're skimming across the surface of April's world, and you have no idea how treacherous the waters run."

"She's not the only one who's had a rough life."

"Fuck you, Cole." Dewey's squeezed his hands into fists. "Don't even compare your shit to hers."

"As the Senator once said, are there different degrees of hell?" Ryan sipped his beer, hoping the cool liquid would chill his building rage. "Thing is, even though I resent the hell out of it, our pasts *are* what connects us. I think we see that deep down we are broken, but together...fuck, I don't know, we find calm or some rainbow la-la shit." What kind of crap was spewing from his mouth? This woman was beginning to mean something to him, and he'd be damned if he'd let Dewey come in here and warn him off. Off what? He didn't want to contemplate the answer, because whatever it was had already dug its spurs into his heart.

Dewey blew out a long breath. "Her calm will end when you leave."

"You can't know that." Ryan shot out of the chair, barely refraining from throwing his half-empty bottle against the wall. "She'll be fine. I won't abandon her completely. Did you ever consider that perhaps I can't leave her now? That I need to save her?"

"You will likely move to the East Coast. The senator *is* very influential, after all." Dewey crossed his bulky arms over his chest.

"You'll be busy with college then a new career. How do you plan on maintaining your friendship? She isn't up on social interaction. I mean, she just recently got a phone. She reads. That's it. And now, she spends time with you."

"So, I'll start preparing her." The thought of leaving her had kept him up the past couple nights, because this summer-scheme was coming to an end. They had five weeks left. Or maybe he liked to think he only had five weeks left so then he wouldn't have to deal with his confusing emotions.

"I understand, in the end, I have no say in this matter. Senator David will do as he pleases. I just needed to come by and say my piece. April isn't a science experiment, or whatever it is you two are doing. She's a lost girl trying to find herself, and if she loses ground because of you, I swear, I will find you, and I will kick your ass." After delivering that message, Dewey stomped out, slamming the door behind him.

Ryan stared after him. Life was full of doors. Some closed, some opened, some he knocked on, some he kicked open, and some...some he bolted shut and never opened again. He had no idea what was on the other side of April's door, or even his own. She had improved, and he was proud of her growing confidence. But Dewey was right. What happened when he left her behind? Why did the door have to shut completely? Why couldn't she come East with him? They *were* studying the same thing. Was he actually contemplating a relationship with April? When had that happened?

He drained his beer, emptied and tossed Dewey's, and then hit the fridge for another. Surely this puzzle would become clearer in a haze of alcohol. Yet, three beers in, and he still had only questions. He didn't really know April. That woman had as many closed doors as he did. The only difference was, he could barrel through his—the question of the hour remained, could she do the same?

CHAPTER 6

In the teashop's storeroom, Ryan grabbed a sleeve of to-go cups off the top shelf. Jones probably wouldn't appreciate him having a friend in the back, but Lori had stormed past the barriers, as usual.

"Where have you been lately?" Lori asked for the second time, obviously hoping he'd have a different answer.

He glanced over his shoulder. Seemed leggy blondes were his weakness. Only this blonde was covered in colorful tattoos with piercings in interesting places. Lori was his when-the-mood-struck friend with benefits. Although, before meeting April, Lori had been benefitting a lot, which had him worrying she was thinking commitment. Her tendency to kick up a fuss each time some chick spoke to him across the bar was reason enough to put the brakes on any sort of relationship. Clingy women who had expectations, didn't do it for him, which was why her showing up today grated on his nerves.

"Lori, I'm working. Why don't you come by my place tonight before our shift at Galaxy, and we'll have a quick bite?"

"You are *not* blowing me off again." She shook her head, her straight hair, brushing against her shoulders.

Much different than another blonde whose hair fell in waves. Waves he longed to run his fingers through.

"Earth to Ryan." Lori punched his shoulder. "What's going on? Why are you working in a teashop, for God's sake?"

"I told you months ago that continuing school was my top priority. I won't work as a bartender forever."

She huffed and crossed both arms over her chest. "So, going back to school means you don't hang with your friends anymore?"

"I'm not rehashing my life, my decisions, my anything right now." Frowning, he brushed past her, storming toward the front counter while checking the clock on the wall. *Shit.* Ten minutes until April arrived. "Listen, Lori, seriously, I'm at work. I don't have time for whatever this is."

Tapping her flip-flop clad toe, she simply glared.

The bells on the front door jangled and chimed

April walked in, but stopped when she glimpsed Lori behind the counter. Her hands started working, likely unsettled by the tableau before her. And what in the world was she so dressed up for? Was she wearing makeup? Her features seemed even more defined, and that fitted green dress did a lot of defining on its own.

Ryan's heart raced for whatever stupid reason. No, he knew the reason. April had him all flipped around—in his head and in his heart. He wasn't like this. Didn't want to care. Liked his carefree lifestyle. Enjoyed women like Lori. In helping April find her path, he'd lost his own. He took a deep breath and faced Lori. "I have a customer, so unless you want to order something, I suggest you go."

Lori flicked her gaze to April then back to him before narrowing her eyes. "I just bet you'd like me to leave." She waved a hand toward April. "Who is that?"

A violent emotion stirred within, calling on his need to protect the weak. He cared about Lori, always had, always would, but April wasn't capable of fending for herself if Lori switched to back-off-my-man mode.

Lori stepped around him and braced her hands on the

counter. "What is it you want?"

April frowned. "Tea."

Biting his bottom lip, Ryan refrained from laughing. She always took everything so literally.

"Yeah, I bet," Lori scoffed.

April took a few more steps toward the counter. "Are you working here now?"

Yep, her nerves were on full display, because she was using her auditorium voice. They'd discussed this issue, but obviously April-megaphone-pants came out in stressful situations.

Lori shrank back. "Why are you shouting?"

Ryan shoved Lori behind him. "April, go sit, please. I'll get your tea in a minute."

April bit her bottom lip. "But, Ryan, I cannot stay. I'm getting my hair cut." She tugged on her thick blonde strands.

She peered at him with those big blue eyes and all he could think about was how she'd be cutting off all those locks before he'd had a chance to touch them. Before they were spread across his pillow, all mussed from sex and an overabundance of friction. "Just how much are you getting cut?"

"Oh...not much. Cheri, my father's...um...girlfriend showed me pictures in a magazine, and she's waiting outside. We have an appointment. She's very excited, but I told her I had to have my tea first, because you might worry if I didn't show up. Cheri even wanted me to get her some tea. She said something green, and I said you would help me pick it out. So, I can't wait very long, or I might miss my appointment."

Lori had remained at his side and simply stared. "What are you talking about? What is she talking about?" She glanced at Ryan. "*This* is who you've dumped me for? I get that she's pretty, but she's missing a few springs upstairs."

"That's enough." Ryan gripped Lori's arm and tugged her toward the back.

"Wait." April stepped closer and leaned over the counter.

"Are you Ryan's friend, too?"

"His friend? Oh, no. I'm a hell of a lot more than that." Lori's tone went feral. "What is your damage, sister? Your innocent flower shit doesn't play. Ryan doesn't do girls like you."

Great. He'd be responsible for April's first catfight. Dewey would owe him an ass kicking for this, too.

April raised a single brow. "I assume the word *do*"—she flashed up air quotes with her fingers—"means sex?"

Ryan's mouth gaped open. What in the world was April doing? He glanced at her sweet face, only this time he noted a wicked gleam in her eyes. One he'd never seen before. The look spoke of a sneaky mock-innocence. The little devil knew exactly what she was saying. Unfortunately, Lori spoke with her fists. So, he dragged her off before she jumped the counter and destroyed his woman.

"That." Lori jabbed a finger toward April. "*She* is your new thing? What the fuck, Ryan? What's wrong with her? Is she re—"

"Don't you dare say that word." He yanked her toward the back door. "We've been friends for a long time, but if you say that word, we're done. Nothing is wrong with her. She's just..." He raked his fingers through his hair. Lost, so lost. "Listen, I won't discuss her. Now, I've got to see if she's all right."

"Ryan, I deserve more than this."

Lori's tone had him contemplating his whole, was-he-a-good-person conundrum again. She *did* deserve an explanation. "Fine." He sighed. "You're right. I'm sorry. Just give me a minute." He left a bewildered Lori behind, and with each step, he also left behind a piece of his past. This craving for April, the need for her friendship, her smiles, that intoxicating rose fragrance, her intelligence, had all bamboozled his heart and left him...where?

He had to take Dewey's warnings to heart. He couldn't develop this relationship with April any further. They were friends. Actually, he was a *paid* friend. He had to push her more, maybe even suggest social outlets other than himself, like a book club or a gym. Not that she wasn't extremely healthy. *Do not think about her body.* Don't mentally draw her perfect curves and long, slender fingers. Something about her hands drove him crazy. Who the hell got off thinking about a woman's hands?

When he got to the counter, he frowned. She still stood in the same spot. "April, what are you doing?"

She shrugged before smiling. "I'm waiting for you."

With those words, the fight momentarily stopped. He'd never lied to himself, and he wouldn't start now. Everything he hadn't wanted to feel crashed through his soul and burst through his heart. His whole life he'd fought not to feel, but with her wide, innocent stare, with those bright blue eyes and her ridiculous practically formal dress, her words meant so much more. Did she know? Was she capable of offering him everything he desired? Was his dream one-sided?

Furious his emotions remained a jumbled mess and she stood there in a curve-enhancing green dress, he snapped, "What the hell are you wearing?"

"Oh, I thought I should dress up to get my hair done." She cleared her throat. "This dress is very fashionable."

Damn it. Why did she have to say such odd shit? He'd practically roared at her, and she just smiled and answered. He wanted to fall on his knees and say, I've been waiting for you, too. But was that right for her? Was she ready? Was he? Their futures were on separate courses, and although he'd likely never forgive himself for not attempting a more meaningful relationship, he had to face reality. So, he inhaled two deep breaths, closed his eyes, and focused on what was best.

"April." He met her gaze. "I need to deal with Lori. Just look at the variety of green teas we have for Cheri. I'll be back as soon as I can."

She rubbed her hands together at her waist.

Oh, shit. For some reason, that wasn't the right answer.

"I don't think that would be a good idea."

Double shit. Her tone was loud again. "Look at me, April."

When she met his gaze, she exhaled visibly.

"What's wrong?"

She glanced toward the wall of teas. "Once I start, I can't stop until I smell them all. I'm sorry."

"What do you mean?"

"I don't know." She hung her head and fiddled with the button along the neckline of her dress.

He cursed. "Sit down. I'll be right back."

She hesitated.

"April. Sit." She glared but then took the two steps to her seat with her chin down as if going to her own beheading. He heaved a sigh then went back to ease things over with Lori. He found her wafting a hand over a vat of lavender-mint tea.

"What was she doing?" Lori closed the tea lid.

"*She's* a customer and having her wait isn't fair, so can we do this tonight?" He gripped Lori's arm and gently squeezed.

She lifted a can of Rooibos tealeaves and studied the label. "I knew you were going to rip my heart out of my chest, but now that you've done it..."

"Lori—"

"Fuck off, Cole and just shut up for a second." Jaw clenched, she leaned against the wall, her gaze on her worn flip-flops. "I don't want your pity, and you never promised me nothing."

"I'm still sorry." Ryan knew saying, I'm sorry was nothing but empty words but he wanted to ease the divide between them.

"I shouldn't have come barging in here. It's just...I-I miss you, and...I wanted...well, I'm worried about you."

She must have been off-kilter, as she never got tongue-tied. "Thanks for worrying about me." Using his index finger, he lifted her chin. "I really do care about you."

"Yeah, right," she scoffed, but her lips lifted a little on the ends. "I hate your new girlfriend, by the way. She's too perfect, and she's weird."

"*I'm* weird, so she fits." He wrapped his arms around her thin frame. "I'm sorry, Lori."

"Don't get all lovey-dovey now, asshole." She huffed out a laugh. "We're still friends though, right? I need that. And, yeah, so maybe I kind of started to like you a little. Big mistake." She nestled into his arms. "I won't cry for long, because I'm kinda interested in this redheaded moron who keeps coming into the bar. He's asked me out a few times. He's like you though, a complete idiot."

"If he is an idiot, he'll answer to me."

"So, we're officially in the friend-zone with no sex?"

"Yeah, I'm afraid so."

"Damn it."

He chuckled. "Oh, you have no idea."

CHAPTER 7

Slippery from sweat, Ryan growled when his sunglasses slid down his nose. Again. Cursing, he used the bottom of his T-shirt to wipe his face. He'd needed this walk to clear his head and, though hot, the weather wasn't all that steamy—he'd had enough of steamy.

The past two nights at Galaxy, he'd turned down a slew of offers for meaningless sex. Ladies always wanted the bartender. Perhaps the attraction was the prospect of free drinks, or maybe the mystique of the bad boy. Though, not all bartenders ran around fucking everything in sight. Not that he hadn't lived up to the stereotype the first couple years of his employment...and yeah, for quite a while after that, but he *did* have needs and he *had* been careful. However, those oat-sowing tendencies had settled lately. The nights of wild abandon less frequent.

What did April think about the workings between men and women? Sometimes, he'd catch her observing him. Was she interested in him as more than a friend?

Perhaps he was just overdue for a long night of sweaty sex, but he was careening dangerously close to wanting her on a physical level, and he'd rather not be the only one crashing. Yet, she had a very negative reaction to touch, so his lustful fantasies were likely going nowhere. The idea of him with Senator Paul

David's daughter was ludicrous anyway.

On his way back from lunch with Charlie, Galaxy's owner, Ryan glanced into the cupcake shop across the street and caught a flash of shiny blonde hair. He'd been on his way home to catch up on sleep before heading back to work, but seeing April somewhere other than the tea shop and library was more temptation than he could bear. He crossed the street and peered into the window. There she sat all-look-but-don't-touch, because a guy like him couldn't afford to taste the delights behind the glass.

In front of her were six different cupcakes, and two cartons of white milk. Next to them on the table was a pink baker's box. She seemed mesmerized by the swirled mounds of icing.

The bell on the door jingled as he pressed it open. Cool air blasted across his face, and he stopped to breathe it in for a moment. Ah...air conditioning.

April didn't look up.

Maybe she couldn't hear his approach. Unable to resist, he slid into the seat across from her. Eyes wide, her head shot up but then she smiled, all teeth and joy-filled gleam.

He started to smile back then frowned when he saw the tears on her cheeks. *What the hell?* Most people would be ecstatic with six cupcakes. They each had a tiny nibbled area, as if a mouse had feasted upon them. Upon closer study, April had a bit of chocolate on the side of her mouth. The fact he couldn't lick it off added to his growing sexual frustration. "What's going on here, April?"

She blinked. "Hello, Ryan."

"What's with the cupcake explosion?"

"They aren't falling apart." She furrowed her brow. "What do you mean? Are you referring to all my cupcakes?"

"Yes." He refrained from rolling his eyes at her literal interpretation. "Why are you sad?"

"Today is my birthday." Her voice pitched low, almost a whisper.

"I see. So, you decided to celebrate with six cupcakes. Are you sad because you can't eat just one?" He flipped the chair around and rested his arms across the back. "I say finish them all." He nodded toward the cupcakes. "Which one did you like best?"

"I walk by here all the time, and I think someday I'm going in there and trying every single flavor." She fingered a sugar butterfly candy. "They are so pretty."

"They are. A bit too much icing, though."

"Father couldn't come back from Washington today, so I decided I would try the cupcakes. Maria says chocolate is the cure for everything."

"She's right." He chuckled but then thoughts of his own lonely birthdays surfaced. No cake. No presents. No parents. Shaking his head, he cleared those unpleasant memories from his mind. "Who is Maria?"

"She is the housekeeper's helper." She leaned close and whispered, "She and Dewey are dating, but it's a secret."

"Okay, I won't tell anyone." He made a show of crossing a finger over his heart. The sugary scents from the cupcakes combined, with her enticing floral bouquet, had him wishing to feast at her feet forever. "Where is Dewey anyway?"

"He went to visit his friend who works at the butcher shop."

The guy was probably down there talking protein shakes with some other muscle-laden dude. Although, he should appreciate Dewey more as he seemed to be April's only friend. "How old are you anyway? And you never answered my question, which cupcake is best?"

"I'm twenty-one, and I think I like the lemon one, but the caramel chocolate is good, too."

"Twenty-one? And you're lining up cupcakes instead of shots?"

"Shots?"

Likely she'd only had wine on special occasions. At this milestone, she should be living it up with a crazy group of friends and doing lots of things she'd regret in the morning. He'd volunteer to be at the top of that list. *Not going to happen, Cole.* "What's in here?" He tapped the top of the pink box.

"Oh, I'm sorry. Would you like a cupcake?" She lifted the lid. "I bought twelve."

"Sure, let me see what you've got."

Her smile went a mile wide as she explained each cupcake as though she'd worked in a bakery for years. He patiently listened and let her talk him into eating two. The sugar overload burned his tongue, but in a good way. He'd need a gallon of bitter coffee to wash down everything.

"If I'm eating these, then you need to finish a couple of yours, too." He flicked a finger toward her row of cupcakes. "Don't be wasteful."

She smiled then lifted the yellow one.

"So, your dad is out of town on your birthday?"

She bit into the mound of icing then licked her lips.

Watching her pink tongue, Ryan cleared his throat and shifted in his seat. "Uh…is that why you were sad?"

Her face crumpled a bit, her enjoyment of all the sugar melting away. "Part of it."

His fingers itched to touch her lips. To hold her until she smiled again. "What's the other part?"

She shrugged.

"April. Tell me."

"Ugh…you're so bossy. Dr. Ashburn says so too." She sniffed and drank from her milk before sighing deeply. "My father isn't here. My mother is dead. I was feeling lonely. That's all."

"My father isn't here, either." Why those words left his mouth, he'd never be able to say. He never spoke about his father. To anyone. Ever.

Pity shone in her eyes. "Really? I'm sorry."

"I'm not. Fucker's in jail."

"You cuss a lot."

To keep his mouth busy, he dug into a third cupcake. "You should come to the bar tonight. I'll buy you a round of real shots, with a bit less sugar." He offered the invitation with his mouth full of chocolate icing, knowing she'd never agree.

"What bar?"

He coughed, still wishing he had something to drown all this sweetness. "Galaxy. It's up the street."

"What do you do there?" She folded her empty cupcake wrapper. Then placed the perfectly folded triangle on top of a napkin.

"I'm a bartender."

"All right, then." Squaring her shoulders, she tapped the table with her knuckles.

He paused with the last bite of cupcake by his lips. "All right then, what?"

"I'll come to your bar for my birthday."

"April, have you ever even had alcohol? Let alone been to a bar? Or even a restaurant?" He winced. He might have revealed a little too much by asking those questions, but he doubted she'd become suspicious.

"A bar, no, but I've seen them on TV and movies. I think I will attend." She nodded decisively.

This was the worst idea he'd ever had, but he couldn't back out now, because that would hurt her feelings. While true, he did believe she needed to get out more, throwing her to the Galaxy wolves wasn't quite what he'd meant. "From what I can tell about you, I don't think you'll be comfortable around a large crowd. On Saturday nights, the bar is wall-to-wall people. The music is insane. People are dancing, sometimes they jump on the bar. Fights break out." He paused to take a breath.

She reached across the table and took his hand.

Normally, she shrank away. The gentle press of her fingers left him temporarily speechless.

"Ryan, I haven't told you something. Well, actually, a lot of somethings, but this one is relevant for now."

Oh, honey, I already know it all.

"My father sat me down and said I had to become more independent. I have tried very hard to do so. I have certain…issues that keep me from being normal. Or the way most people view normal." With her free hand, she fiddled with the lip of her milk carton. "I know I am different. I don't like it, but I'm trying to change. Perhaps, if I attend your bar, I can observe women my own age, and I'll have a better understanding of how to behave."

He pulled her hand closer, and then lined his fingers with hers before locking them together. "April…I *like* that you are different. Nothing is wrong with who you are. I think it's great you're becoming more independent. I'm not sure why you've been so sequestered, but I don't believe a bar is the best place to find role models."

"But you said you would buy me shots." Her blue eyes held his, holding tons of unasked questions.

"I was joking."

"I see." Her lower lip jutted out.

"Damn it. Fine." He squeezed her hand, wondering if all the sugar had affected his brain. "But you *will* sit at the bar where I can keep an eye on you."

"Really?" Smiling, she practically wiggled in her seat. "Oh, thank you, Ryan. What time should I attend?"

What time should she attend? She spoke as if preparing for a charity gala. Still, they had to experiment with these types of adventures.

He explained what time and where to enter and what to say. Then he grabbed her box of half-eaten treats, walked her home, and placed a desperate call to Dewey.

CHAPTER 8

As predicted, the bar was seven types of crazy. Worrying about April had Ryan's grouch-factor so high even the furry green Oscar hid inside his junky metal can. Galaxy was down one waitress, which meant more people crowding the bar, plus he'd already broken up one catfight, and he had the scratches to prove it.

Dewey had texted five minutes ago, saying they were on their way.

Birthday shots. What had he been thinking? He'd already dropped two beer bottles and messed up one whiskey sour due to dwelling on his insane invitation.

But, the whole way back to her father's place, April had gone on and on about visiting a bar, and how she'd for sure bring her license. He'd refrained from mentioning perhaps she should do something about her clothes. Management would likely frown upon him smacking the shit out of someone for making fun of her even though he'd basically done the same.

His mood ranged from excitement to utter fear. What if he'd pushed her too far? She barely tolerated being around other people as it was, and now she was on the verge of a wild Saturday night at Galaxy? *Brilliant, Cole, just brilliant.*

He'd worked here for four years and never once had he

asked Jack, the bouncer, to put a name on the pass list.

Jack had smirked but scribbled down April and Dewey's names.

Ryan glanced toward the door, and his stomach churned as he saw Dewey's tall form weaving through the crowd. He'd reserved a stool for April right in front of the beer taps, since he spent the majority of his evening there. His heart skipped a beat when he caught a glimpse of shiny blonde hair, rolling in wavy curls around her face, falling onto her shoulders.

A Hispanic girl held April's hand, leading her forward.

He'd known April was tall, but when her legs were wrapped in tight denim, that length took on a whole new meaning. Then her tiny blue shirt barely covered her mid-riff and highlighted a chest that had apparently been hidden underneath all her homely attire.

What. The. Fuck.

Now his heart thundered with lust and exasperation at the same time.

She caught his eye and smiled.

Done. He was so done.

Without any embellishments on her pure face she was beautiful enough, but add a little lipstick and mascara, and the woman became a siren.

"Damn it." He pulled an overflowing beer glass from under the spout.

April waved madly as she made her way closer.

Dewey looked less than pleased, and the gal, who must have been Maria, swayed to the music as she walked beside April.

He ignored everyone flashing cards and cash and waited for April to sit, because until she was where she belonged he couldn't function.

"Hi, Ryan." Her loud voice actually worked quite well here. "Ryan, this is Maria. She let me wear her shirt tonight, because she said I had no bar clothes, and she said I should wear a Mustang's shirt since they are a popular sports team."

Almost speechless, he nodded at Maria and spit out, "Nice to meet you." What he wanted to do served cross-purposes. On one hand, he wanted to fall to his knees and thank Maria for choosing such a revealing shirt. On the other, he didn't want anyone getting the wrong idea about his woman.

And, though he was working for April's father, lying about his purpose in her life, he went ahead and jumped into happy-rainbow-Care-Bear land, admitting she *was* his woman. Her father might be absent from April's life on her birthday, but the senator had given her a gift—him. "You look real nice, birthday girl. I didn't realize you were bringing a friend, or I would've saved another stool." He waved a hand at the reserved seat, and April settled in.

A regular, Kevin, took in April with a sleazy once-over. "I'll move for her friend."

"Kevin." Ryan narrowed his eyes. "Quit staring."

"Fine," Kevin mumbled, tossing some cash on the bar. "I'll see you later."

Once he left, Maria slid into his vacant seat.

Realizing he needed to calm his shit, Ryan took a deep breath then smiled at April. "What can I get you, beautiful?"

Dewey closed in behind her and settled both hands on the back of Maria's chair. "We'll take two Sam Adams drafts, and April will have a Shirley Temple."

Eyes narrowed, Dewey seemed to dare him to make a comment. Grateful to the big guy for taking a chance on this outing, Ryan simply nodded. "Good choice."

April flashed a wide grin and then turned to stare out over the crowd. When done, she faced Dewey and some unspoken communication passed between them.

Ryan placed the bubbly pink drink before April. "We'll get you something stronger if you feel like it later. Right now, enjoy this, okay?"

She cupped a hand against her left ear. "What?"

"Drink this." He shouted, realizing she probably had a hard time hearing him above all the meshing sounds.

"I don't usually drink soda." She wrinkled her nose. "Too much sugar."

Ryan winked. "Well, you're twenty-one, live a little."

"Thank you. I will."

Dear God, how was he supposed to work and fight off all the assholes who'd undoubtedly hit on her all night? He cursed his earlier sugar-induced high, which had him spewing ridiculous invitations to a woman who deserved candlelight, not strobe lights.

Damn cupcakes.

# # #

Between pouring drinks and lining up shots for the Saturday night patrons, Ryan stopped and chatted with April each time he poured a draft. She seemed to enjoy talking to him and Maria. Dewey hadn't cracked a smile, and though Maria had ordered two more beers, he'd stuck with only one.

April spent most of the night wide-eyed, staring all around.

And then *he* showed up, Ryan should have expected his appearance, since he owned the place and wasn't playing tonight.

Tall, blond, all-American good looks. Charlie Summers. The quarterback for the Indianapolis Mustangs, and of course, the bastard would notice the most beautiful woman in the room.

Charlie elbowed up to the bar and slid alongside April.

Dewey shot him a dirty look then his eyebrows went sky high after realizing who was bumping into his charge.

Ryan meandered down the bar, filling a few drink orders as he went. He caught a glimpse of April smiling and nodding at Charlie, and then she pointed in his direction.

Charlie looked his way and shook his head.

Ryan smirked, ignored a request from a redhead to do a couple shots, and scooted down the bar. "What's up, Chuck?"

"Fuck you."

"Never gets old."

"Yes…yes, it does."

"Whatcha need, man?" Ryan tapped his fist against the bar.

"Usual, and get April another round of whatever she's drinking."

Charlie stared down at April with a grin that didn't bode well at all. If he kept leering like that, Ryan would be forced to blacken his lips. "So, you've met *my* April."

"I have."

"April." Ryan leaned against the bar.

"Yes?" She turned slightly so her left ear was closer.

"Do you watch much football?"

"Football?" Her blonde brows furrowed, and she tapped a slender index finger against her plump lips. "No, I don't watch sports, but Father and Dewey do. Why do you ask?"

"No reason." Ryan smirked at Charlie, who merely shrugged.

"May I have a drink with actual alcohol this time? You said I could have shots, remember?" April glanced at Charlie. "He and Dewey think I do not know I have a child's drink." She rolled those beautiful blue eyes.

"Don't you think you should take baby steps?" Ryan opened the cooler then slid Charlie his usual beer choice.

"I'm not a baby." April gripped a cocktail napkin in her hand, crumpling it.

"No, you definitely are not," Charlie piped up, giving her another thorough once-over.

Ryan grabbed Charlie's beer off the counter. "Go flirt with someone else."

"Hey, I wasn't done with that."

"Yes, you were." Ryan made a show of pouring the bottle's

contents down the drain. "April, look at me." He waited until she met his gaze. "I have something special planned for later. After I clock out, I'll grab a bottle of champagne, and we can head up to my apartment."

"Dewey says we have to leave at eleven. I only have fifteen more minutes."

"Who's Dewey?" Charlie arched a brow.

Dewey turned at the sound of his name. "I am."

"Damn, you're a big one. You play ball?"

"Yes."

"Where?"

While Dewey and Chuck recalled their glory days, Ryan slid April another drink—without alcohol. "Maybe he'll let you stay, and I can take you home."

She folded her hands together on top of the bar, knuckles white. "I don't know where you live, Ryan."

"Basically, just across the street. In the apartments."

"Oh."

"Oh?" He wiped his hands on a bar rag. "What's that mean?"

"I've never gone to a man's house before."

That caught Charlie's attention; he shot Ryan a what-the-fuck look.

Before the big quarterback could question anything, Ryan jumped in, "Charlie, I had a question about the vodka stock, could you come back here for a minute?"

"Yeah, sure."

"April, I'll be right back. Talk to Dewey about staying with me." He winked, asked the waitress to stand in for a few minutes, and then headed toward the back office.

Once inside the room, Charlie pulled up the night's sales reports from the computer. "What am I back here for, Ryan? I know it's not the vodka stock."

"That's the girl I was telling you about."

"No shit. I thought you said she was deaf."

"Partially."

"Interesting." He rubbed his chin. "Well, there *is* something about her...she's as beautiful as you said. But...you sure you want to get involved? That's not a quick fuck right there, that's long term."

"I've done the quick fuck, the long fuck, every fuck, but nah...I'm done. She and I...something's right. My past, her past, we even each other out."

"I can't make that determination, since you didn't say much about her other than who her father was and that she needed a friend."

Ryan shrugged.

"Tell ya what, go ahead and take off for the night. I'll pull the boys in, and we'll do a celebrity bartender night. Women love that shit."

"Yeah?" Ryan studied his friend. The guy was doing him a solid, always had really, and he should appreciate that more. He clapped Charlie on the back. "Thanks, man."

Charlie raised a brow. "*That* blonde is some supermodel-slash-penthouse shit, right there. Those lips and those eyes. Fuck me."

"She's amazing."

"Amazing?"

"Yeah."

"You *are* gone if you're using pussy words like *amazing*."

"I cannot wait until you meet an amazing woman, and *you* puss out."

"Might as well. My whole team has fallen under the spell of pussy-itis. I'm sure I'm next. That kind of bad juju spreads like the plague."

"All right, well, if you're taking over the bar then I'm out. I'm taking a bottle of sparkling wine from the back."

Charlie pulled out his phone and started texting. "I'll notify the boys."

For April

Ryan glanced at Charlie's phone, laughed at the colorful verbiage, and then took off before his buddy changed his mind.

CHAPTER 9

With a pink bottle of sparkling wine in his hand, Ryan headed around the outside of the bar's counter and clambered over to where April was in a heated discussion with Dewey.

"Hey, what's wrong?" He grasped her shoulder.

She stiffened so he removed his hand.

Her cheeks were flushed and both hands were planted on her hips. "I can't go. Dewey says I was allowed to come tonight and that was enough."

Ryan faced Dewey. "Let's go across the street and talk this through. It's too loud in here."

"No." Dewey shook his head. "You wanted her here. She came. She's not staying over at your place. That wasn't part of the deal."

The way he said *deal* made clear he was referencing more than just tonight. "I disagree."

"Do you?"

"If April wants to stay at my place for a bit, why shouldn't she?"

"I could mention a whole lot of whys."

Maria took Dewey's arm. "Let's compromise. We'll go with them. Besides, April only turns twenty-one once."

Dewey wiped a hand over his chin. "Fine, but we are *not* staying long."

That said he stormed toward the door.

Ryan followed. Not really caring how long Dewey *thought* they were staying. The man hadn't seen how lonely April was earlier. They would help her celebrate by having a few drinks of this bubbly swill. Everyone deserved a little alcohol on their twenty first birthday. And sparkling wine was tame enough.

He'd even tidied his place in the hope she'd agree to visit. Seemed ridiculous a woman her age couldn't make her own decisions, but he understood Dewey's concerns. Ryan probably shouldn't be trusted with her. He wanted to do things to her, with her, all over her that would likely scare her. Still, he wanted a private opportunity to ask if she was interested in exploring an intimate relationship.

She'd likely never been intimately kissed or touched. A condition he'd remedy soon, even if a little manipulation was involved.

"April, can I hold your hand?" Just outside the bar's door, he held out his hand—waiting and hoping.

"Yes." Closing her fingers over his, she didn't flinch, just smiled and squeezed his hand.

#

"Would you like more wine?"

"No." Holding her half-empty glass, April stood and began pacing in front of the living room window, wringing her hands. "Why did you want me to stay?"

"I wanted to ask you something in private." A privacy hard won. He'd finally convinced Dewey to give them two hours. Actually, April had declared she would stay by telling Dewey this was her birthday present. Dewey had tugged him into the kitchen, threatened his life, and then stormed out. Maria had waved goodbye and followed.

April faced him. "It's raining outside, and I don't have an umbrella."

"I want to ask you something, so, come here." Ryan patted the sofa beside him.

"I-I am afraid of what you'll ask me, because I think I know." Head bent, she studied the tips of her shoes, her tiny shirt rising to reveal her pale belly as she sighed.

"Don't be afraid."

She glanced out the window once more then crossed the room and sat beside him.

"May I hold your hand again?"

"Yes, but I don't usually like to be touched."

"I've kind of picked up on that." Winking, he took her hand and folded their fingers together. "You've got me all messed up inside."

Her cheeks turned a light shade of pink. "I'm sorry."

"No. It's a good thing." He shifted in his seat, unsure how he'd explain what he wanted. Talking, feelings, the whole thing was out of his comfort zone...but he'd do it for her. "The only way to say this is to just spit it out, so here goes. April, I'm very attracted to you, and I understand that may frighten you. I'm unclear on the source of your fears, but I want you to know, I'm okay with whatever the reason may be. I will never force myself upon you. I'll always ask. Now, if you only want to be friends, I'll accept that, too."

Taking a deep breath, she glanced at him before dropping her gaze to their joined hands. "Ryan, I have...you see, I'm not like other women. My story...who I am is not something any man could ever understand or accept, so I believe we should remain friends. I am not like those women at the bar." Her shoulders drooped. "At times I wish I could be, but I'm just too different. And you don't deserve different, you deserve a woman who isn't afraid to be touched. Who doesn't need medication just to get out of bed some days."

Ryan considered asking about her medications, but then decided he needed to stay focused on her belief they were too different. "You are putting limitations on us, on me, that I do *not* see or believe." Actually, he did understand all the reasons a relationship between them was a huge batch of crazy, but he no longer wanted to fight how he felt, so maybe this convince-April convo was just as much for him as it was for her. "I don't know everything about you, but I do know something awful must have happened for you to be so guarded."

Her blonde hair swished back and forth across her shoulders. "I wasn't isolated, I was institutionalized." She pulled away and stood, gaze darting toward the door.

"Sit back down, please."

"I shouldn't let you boss me around." She sniffed before perching her fine ass on the edge of the couch again.

"Let me try something?"

"Okay."

"May I hold you?"

She nodded and leaned toward him a little, her gaze locked on his lips.

Holding back a smile at her small hint of interest, Ryan wrapped an arm around her shoulders and held her at his side. "Please, listen before you decide."

She slumped in his arms. "I-I'm sorry," she cried. "I wish I could be the girl for you. I get furious with myself when I think I can never have a man in such a way. I'm just now discovering my strength. I don't know how to return your affections. Physical intimacy is…well, my introduction to such things was…not pleasant."

He couldn't help but wonder how unpleasant, but again, he didn't want to get hung up on another subject. "I'd like to tell you why everything you believe about me is wrong."

"No." She stiffened and pressed a hand against his chest. "You are not the one who is wrong, I am."

"Stop. Don't say those things about yourself." He tipped up her chin. "Intimacy doesn't always mean sex. We can start by becoming intimate in a different way. I'll tell you something I've never told anyone before."

"Why?" She sniffed again before glancing around the room, likely looking for a tissue. "Why would you do this for me?"

"Because I'm different, too." He sat up and headed to the kitchen for paper towels. "Only, I wear my weird on the outside." Handing over the whole roll, he settled back on the couch and touched the tattoos lining his arms. "I mark up my body. I push and fight, but you keep everything inside. A serene, untouchable beauty." Easing her back into his arms, he brushed her soft hair behind her pink tipped ear. "I've never been one to stop at posted barriers, so we'll work through our demons together."

After wiping her red eyes and nose, April scoffed. "My demons are scarier than you could ever imagine."

"I'm familiar with scary." He met her gaze for a long moment. "My mom...well, I wasn't able to help her, and she died. I won't go through that again."

"Why would you?"

Did April really not see herself as someone who needed help? Was he wrong in his assessment? Maybe he had their roles reversed? "Let me just tell this story, okay? Now, close your eyes."

She turned to face him, her lips far too close. "Why must I close my eyes?"

"Because I don't want to see your pity."

After a moment, she settled back into place, resting her head against his shoulder. "All right."

"When I finish this story, I'll take you home, and I want you to consider that perhaps we can heal one another. A relationship with a man involves many levels, and you have no reason to be afraid." He caressed her soft, pale cheek. "At your doorstep, I want to kiss you good night, and I'd like you let me."

Her eyes popped open. "Will you use your tongue?"

"Do you want me to?"

She squirmed. "I'm not sure, as long as you aren't mean about it."

Mean? Why would he be mean? Had she witnessed something while imprisoned or at the institution? "I promise I won't be mean." He gave a solemn nod. "I'm telling you this piece of my past, because I want you to understand that, as a teen, I was also a candidate for an institution or a juvenile facility. But my mom couldn't afford it, because she spent all her money on drugs."

"Oh, I'm sorry, Ryan." Her gaze held a hint of pity.

"Let me finish. Close your eyes." He hated her look of sympathy. His past was what it was. Nothing he could do to change it, but because of her, he wanted to learn from the experience and become a better man.

Her lips pursed. "My therapist says the way you speak to me is not nice and that you are trying to dominate me. He thinks all you see is my beauty and that you have bad intentions."

Ryan chuckled. "Your therapist is absolutely right, but you need someone who won't pussyfoot around, because you had a rough life and your father is a senator. Now, are you ready to be quiet?"

"I suppose." After shooting him a slight glare, she closed her eyes again.

His little kitten's fur was fluffing up more often, but then, whose didn't around him? He took a deep breath and rested his head on top of hers. "I grew up on the southeast side of Indianapolis. Only reason I went to school was so I could eat." Memories of that hollow feeling in his stomach still hadn't faded. Now when he ate, he ate healthy and until he was full. "My ma was dating another loser, only he was mean, like nightmare mean. I don't know if she was so much seeing him or that he was stalking her, but she let him. Either way, guy was a bastard, so I stayed away as much as I could, arriving home late at night and showering at the YMCA." He stopped to take a deep breath and noted he'd been rubbing a hand up and down April's arm and she hadn't said a word. *Huh?* Maybe they'd already reached a level of intimacy between them.

She opened one eye. "Is that all?"

He shook his head. "Nope. Eyes closed."

"Okay."

"One day, while I was walking down an alley behind our house, I saw a stray puppy. Tiny, starved thing with a white spot on his nose but the rest of his coat was all black. I sort of adopted him, took him everywhere, and snuck him food from my school lunches. I even brought him home a few times, when the asshole's car wasn't parked out front.

"Of course, when you wander the streets without much food and sleep, you end up sick. Raging with fever, I crashed at home a few days, and my pup stayed with me. I got bad enough I finally had to go to my ma. She was home with the bastard, and I told her I needed medicine. Of course, they didn't want to spend money on doctor bills, so they loaded me up with aspirin and told me to go back to bed. When they came in my room, they saw the puppy. Apparently, the bastard didn't like dogs so he threw him outside, saying, 'I better never see that animal back in the house.'"

April gasped. "Oh, Ryan. I'm sorry."

"Yeah, so am I."

She patted his arm. "You don't have to tell the rest. Dr. Ashburn lets me stop sometimes when I'm recalling something traumatic."

How not pushing past her demons helped her, he had no idea. Made more sense to shove until she reached a breakthrough. Maybe this guy was half in love with her. "I don't want to stop. Listen, okay?"

"I am right *here*. Of course, I'm listening."

"Does your therapist know about your smart mouth?"

"No. I mean…he does think I'm smart, but—"

"Right." *So literal.* He shook his head. "Back to the story…so, I went against ma's boyfriend's wishes regarding the dog. I was very sick but also worried about the little beast. I found him and brought him inside. Ma caught me. We were arguing about the dog when *he* came back. He and my ma got into it, and he started beating her. He had a knife and started cutting her, said unless I killed the dog, he would kill my ma."

April gasped and placed a hand over her mouth. "I don't like this story."

"I don't, either."

"So, d-did you kill the dog?"

Oh, hell his stomach hurt so bad. Why had he chosen this story again? He cleared his throat, searching for the words to continue. That day, that defining moment was so clear, as if he were still there, facing that decision with the bastard breathing down his neck while holding his shivering puppy. "Ma was screaming, her face all bloodied, and the pup was barking like mad. I had to make a choice. But, deep down, I knew he wouldn't really kill my ma. He needed her. Was obsessed with her. So, I said to go ahead and kill her, maybe I'd get sent to a home and wouldn't have to be with either one of them, anymore. Of course, no matter what I said, I wouldn't have won. He took my puppy outside. I-I tried to follow…but the bastard shoved me. As sick as I was, I went down hard and hit my head on a side table. The next time I woke up, I was in a hospital bed. To this day, I don't know if she called or he did. All I know is Ma told me not to bring home strays anymore. I told her the same. After I got home, I went to my room and slammed my door and there, on my bed was my puppy. I couldn't believe it." Throat tight, Ryan took a deep breath and wiped at the stupid tears pouring down his face.

April touched his cheek, wiping away his tears.

"I fell on the bed, and I-I realized he was dead." Ryan grabbed some of the paper towel and wiped his nose. "His throat was slit and his blood had hardened on my black bedspread. I cried. I'd never cried before, not after all the shit my ma did, and the shit I put up with at school, and the fucking men that came in and out of our lives. But that dog, he'd never done nothing to no one, just followed the wrong boy home. So, on that day, I vowed to never bring home another stray. To never believe that something I loved would last. My heart broke, and it never healed. From that day on, I merely survived. My mom eventually died at the hand of one of those men, but I didn't cry. I haven't cared about anyone, even myself, for so long. I partied. I drank. I did drugs, and I barely graduated school. Sure, I decided to straighten up and become a lawyer, but even that I barely cared about. I've let the world around me stay dark, but then I met you, and I thought, damn it, here's another stray pup that needs your care. For the first time I embraced the idea, because I'm not that helpless boy anymore."

And damn it if he didn't cry. More like lost his mind for a while as he wrapped April in his arms and let loose all the tears he'd kept inside for far too long. "I'm sorry…I can't stop."

"It's all right. I'm crying, too." She just held him tight, gripping her hands in his shirt.

After who knew how long, he could finally breathe.

She helped him breathe.

"What was the name of your puppy?" Easing back, she brushed his over-long bangs from his forehead.

"I didn't name it. Just Puppy."

"Puppy was happy, for a time." Eyes filled with tears, April leaned forward and spoke softly in his ear. "He was your friend, and I know what that's like. I'm sure he enjoyed being with you. Don't be sad about Puppy anymore."

"I'll always be sad." He choked out.

"I know." She offered a watery smile. "I'm sorry. Here, take some more paper towels." She tore off a piece and wiped his cheeks. "I will help you, Ryan. I was wrong earlier. I *will* try for more, because I don't like seeing you so sad. I don't know what to do to comfort you." She lightly patted his cheek twice. "Why does the world have to be so cruel?"

"I don't have an answer for that." He'd have to tell her the truth about his agreement with her father soon. Explain his reasons and tell her he was grateful her father had proposed their friendship. They were both the better for it, even though she was turning him into a bawl-baby-sap-face.

"Thank you for telling me your story."

Her serenity nearly killed him sometimes. "Yeah. Sorry I slobbered all over you."

"That doesn't matter." April took his hand and kissed it. "I won't ever tell anyone your story, Ryan. You can trust me."

"Out of anyone I have ever known, I believe this about you and only you. Do you know how absolutely beautiful you are?" He caressed her cheek, feeling more than he had ever felt about anything or anyone. His heart had opened up, and it was practically shining out of his chest. That knowledge only added to his realization that everything had changed because of her.

"I don't like being so pretty, but I can't help it. Father says it's because Mother was such a beauty. I look like her."

He'd actually meant her inner beauty, but he'd go with it for now. "Do you miss your mother?"

"We did everything together, but then…well, we went for a drive…and…and she…well, I am not ready to tell my stories yet. Dr. Ashburn says I would feel lighter if I just let out everything, but why should I tell him when the only person who could ever understand was my mother? I don't wish to tell anyone else."

"Then don't." He tossed his paper towel onto the floor.

"Perhaps, one day, I will tell you a story that hurts me just as you have told me."

"I'd like that, but right now, I should take you home. Don't want Dewey to storm the castle."

April frowned then leaned forward and drank the rest of her sparkling wine. "I like this stuff. It's bubbly on my tongue." She met his gaze. "Do you think you could kiss me now?"

Her tone had gone loud again, matching the thundering beat of his heart. Now? Like alone-on-the-couch now? Like need-to-bury-my-pain-with-deep-kisses now? Didn't need to ask him twice. "Is that what you'd like?" He brushed his thumb across her lower lip.

She shivered, mouth falling open, but she held his gaze. "Yes, please, because I think kissing me will make you feel better."

He barked out a laugh. "Awful sure of yourself."

Her brow furrowed, and she started to speak.

"No." He reached up and cupped her jaw. "Quiet now, because you're right, kissing you *will* make me feel better, along with a whole lot more." Keeping her gaze, he leaned closer and lightly kissed her lips.

Frowning, she pulled back, her head slightly tilted. "No tongue?"

He refrained from laughing. "I'll add some this time."

She nodded and puckered her lips.

Mentally shaking his head at how damn cute she was, he angled his head to the side and pressed against her mouth. Then, with his tongue, he traced the seam of her lips until she opened, and he delved inside.

She touched her tongue to his and his dick practically exploded. Worried he'd lose control, he pulled back far too soon.

"I liked that." April nodded. "My stomach felt funny, and I wanted it to last longer."

Innocent as a fluffy white baby lamb. And she really didn't need to be debauched by a guy like him, but he didn't give a shit. He'd been given a chance with this woman, and he was taking it. "Think about what I said, and if you decide to be more than friends, I'll kiss you longer and whenever…and wherever you want."

"Wherever? Oh." She giggled then licked her lips. "I believe that's blatant manipulation, counselor."

"Yes, and I won't apologize. I'm very, very guilty."

"I will consider your offer, but I should go home now. Will you be all right?" She patted his knee. "Do you need to tell me more stories?"

"I will, just not tonight."

"All right, then." She stood and took his hand.

But it wasn't all right. Tonight, he'd given her more than he'd ever given anyone, and yet their relationship was built on a lie. What happened when she found out? Would she understand? Forgive him? After telling his story, he was emotionally drained, which meant worrying about losing her would have to come another day.

Another day, and another barrier down. He'd started out this mission with the hopes of changing her, but so far, he was the one barely hanging on to who he used to be.

And oddly enough, that was okay.

CHAPTER 10

At his apartment's kitchen sink Monday afternoon, Ryan used an old toothbrush to scrub the oil and grease from under his nails as he waited for Dewey to arrive. He'd worked all morning on Lori's car. She'd needed a quick oil change, and had spent the majority of the time trying to get him to open up about April. She hadn't gotten much, because he was still trying to work through everything himself.

While walking April home Saturday night, she'd asked him not to think of her as stupid. Said that's what she wanted for her birthday. That discussion led to a bit of an argument, because he didn't feel that way at all. She'd disagreed, to which, he'd responded she shouldn't reflect her own opinions onto him. He'd kissed her again, a bit harder than he should have, and told her she was stupid for thinking he thought she was stupid. The woman had merely shaken her head and said he made no sense before leaving him standing alone at her front door.

Guilt ate at him all day on Sunday, and even now. Perhaps he'd been too harsh in his dealings with her, but he knew no other way.

She wasn't the weak one, he was. After everything he dished out, she still came back. The question weighing most on his mind was where they went from here. To know that path, he needed answers. Since he couldn't get them from her, he'd appeal to Dewey. For hours, he'd considered how to handle the man before calling to request a meeting.

A pounding sounded on the door.

"It's open."

"You just let anyone in without checking? Not smart, Cole." Dewey barreled past him, wearing khaki shorts and a white polo shirt.

Ryan ignored the comment. "Get you a drink?"

"No, but you can get to the point."

"Shut the door. I won't take any more of your time than necessary." Ryan rinsed off his hands and dried them with a paper towel. He stepped out of the kitchen and sank onto his recliner, waving a hand at the couch.

"I'll stand." Dewey crossed both arms over his chest.

"Good call." Ryan rolled his eyes. Dude wasn't giving an inch. "I'll get straight to the point. I know you don't agree with the arrangement I have with April's father, however, I feel our friendship has done her some good."

Dewey grunted.

Whether the sound was in approval or not, Ryan had no idea. "Anyway, she and I changed the direction of our relationship Saturday night."

"I don't think so." He shook his head.

"April can make her own decision about that."

"April isn't ready for a guy like you."

Ryan gritted his teeth. Remaining calm was not his forte, but he'd do it for April. "A guy like *me*? Fuck you, Dewey. She's needed a guy like me for a long time. With our somewhat similar backgrounds, I'm the only one who understands her."

"You don't understand shit."

Dewey hadn't moved, and he hadn't changed his expression.

"What don't I understand?" Ryan flicked up a hand. "Explain what I don't know."

"None of her past is your business."

"I disagree."

"She came home and took one of her hour-long showers. I imagine that had something to do with you touching her."

Jolted, Ryan straightened. "What?"

"Exactly. Let me educate you a little," Dewey huffed. "She suffers from a minor form of haphephobia, which is the fear of touching or being touched. Her condition stems from her imprisonment. Another phobia is mysophobia. She fears contamination and germs. Sometimes, she has severe nightmares. Wakes up the whole house with her screams." Dewey shook his head. "These issues have kept her in the house after she returned from the institution. She only ate certain foods, constantly washed her hands, and she flinched any time someone tried to touch her. Over the past couple years, she's gotten better, but she isn't one-hundred percent."

Pieces of April started to fit together, though he'd observed a few of her personality quirks on his own. Were phobias quirks? He had no idea. And why hadn't her father alerted him to these issues so he wasn't touching her or trying to shove pastries down her throat at the teashop? "Thank you for telling me."

"You can shove that thank you up your sanctimonious ass, Cole. You think this is some kind of game, like Jenga? You build up all the pieces? Well, guess what, those pieces are predisposed to fall. And fall she will."

"You have little faith in someone you *claim* to care about." Ryan folded his hands in his lap, refraining from choking the guy.

"Don't." Dewey raged forward, jabbing a finger in his face. "Don't even act like you care."

"I don't have to act." Ryan kept his gaze locked on Dewey's, not backing down.

"It's all a lie." Dewey kicked the coffee table out of the way and paced back and forth.

"Not anymore." Glancing at the table then back at Dewey,

Ryan arched a brow. "Listen, I plan on telling her the truth. I need some guidance, though. I'm not sure what to say, and you're right, I don't know how to handle her reaction if she becomes…upset."

"You have no right to tell her anything. Leave it alone. You're leaving anyway, right? Don't start something…just…just don't. She's been hurt enough." Dewey crumpled onto the sofa, bracing an elbow against his knee and gripping his forehead in his open palm. "Do you know what I did before coming here?"

"No."

"I picked up her prescriptions. Five bottles, all helping her function."

"Oh…" Five bottles. *Shit!* "Someday, she might not need so many meds."

"Or she might need another after some asshole breaks her heart."

"Her heart's already broken."

"This is true." Dewey nodded then shook his head. "Say I give you the benefit of the doubt. What's your plan?"

"We both want to study law. No reason we can't study together."

"And where is she supposed to do this?"

"She'll come with me."

"Baaammmp." Dewey made a sound like he'd punched a game show buzzer. "Wrong answer. Her home is her safe place. She won't leave with you."

"After a time, I believe she will."

"Cole, you've known her like a month. You have no clue."

"But *you* do, and that's why I asked you here." Ryan gave up being nice and let Dewey have it, practically shouting down the roof. "Instead of throwing up roadblocks, like every other person in April's life, help *me*, help *her*. You say you care so much, but you, and everyone else in her life, fight to keep her the same. She wants to break free. Why won't you let her? She's braver than you and me. Why can't you see that?"

Dewey shoved off the couch and went to stare out the window. "You sound like Maria." He braced both hands on his hips. "I don't want to hold April back...I don't, but I've seen her at her worst. She's different now, but I-I...I'm scared she'll become that hollow creature again." He shivered. "I have nightmares about those days." He turned and met Ryan's gaze. "Have you thought about what it was like to actually live through those events? All of that pushed her over an edge. She's crawled back up, but right now you've got her suspended, hanging onto nothing but a crumbling ledge." He heaved a sigh. "Would you even give a shit if it wasn't for the money?"

Ryan shot out of his chair, bracing his legs apart. "Fuck the money and fuck you."

"Back off. You don't want to fight me."

"I don't? Cause right now, I'm pretty sure I do." Ryan took a step toward Dewey.

"I may have been out of line." Dewey held up a hand. "But, April is *my* family, and I'll be there to pick up the pieces when she falls."

Seriously? If the big guy didn't want to fight him then he needed to shut his fucking mouth. "She will not fall," Ryan gritted out.

Dewey studied him for a moment then headed for the door. One hand on the knob, he glanced over his shoulder. "If she does fall, you'll go down with her."

"Tell me something I don't know, asshole."

Dewey merely grunted in response and then left.

Ryan stared at the door for a long moment, trying to calm his raging anger. He'd gotten his answers, didn't mean he had to like them.

CHAPTER 11

Ten a.m. came and went on Tuesday, and April hadn't showed. Was that her answer to his offer of a deeper relationship? Patience had never been one of his virtues. He'd stomp over to her townhouse and bang on the door if she didn't show on Thursday. They only had so much time left before the start of the next semester. A semester that might have him over nine hundred miles away.

Faced with no prospects for the afternoon except a full load of laundry, he stuck around the teashop, refusing to admit he was actually waiting. After serving a gaggle of giggling high school girls, he decided his eye-twitch just might require medical attention. Done with lingering, he tossed his apron in the dirty clothes bin and glanced at the clock right as it ticked past noon.

The bell on the door jingled.

There she was.

And damn it, if his heart didn't slide out of his body and hop like a giddy dog at her feet. After that ridiculous mental image, Ryan remembered she'd made him wait. "We stopped serving Earl Grey two hours ago."

"That's all right, I don't want Earl Grey."

"No?" He swiveled around.

"No." She padded over to the counter, wearing skinny jeans and a plain white V-necked T-shirt. "I want to order a to-go cup of Ryan Cole."

"You think I'm on the menu?" He held back a smirk. Barely.

"Yes." Her hands fiddled together by her waist.

He decided to give her a break, yet felt he had to be clear. "There are no refunds, do you understand?"

"May I come around the counter like your other friend? The blonde woman?"

"No." He held her gaze.

"Why not?" April frowned.

"Answer the question."

She bit her lower lip. "By saying there are no refunds, you mean I can't change my mind about our relationship, right? Because, when I said I wanted to order you, I thought I was being clear in my wishes."

He nodded. "You're right. You rarely say things you don't mean."

"Were you teasing me about the Earl Grey?"

"Yes." He smiled and hopped onto the counter.

"What are you doing?" She released a slight squeak and stepped back. "I'd like some tea now."

"Oh no, no choosing the grand earl over me." He jerked a thumb at his chest. "You said you wanted a cup of Ryan Cole, so here you go."

Feet shuffling, she stared at the ground. "Don't people hug in moments like these?"

Considering what Dewey had said about her phobia, he held his arms out wide, letting her decide whether or not she wanted to step closer.

She rushed into his arms, practically knocking him over.

He chuckled, wrapping her tight before twirling her around and around. After he set her down, he tweaked her nose. "I was worried when you didn't show up, but I'm glad you're here now.

Glad I waited."

"Can you wait even more?" She held her hands over his shoulders for a moment before lowering them and giving him a slight squeeze. "I've never done anything like this before, and I'm frightened. I started to leave the house so many times today, but then I stopped, and I would get so angry with myself."

He brushed her hair over her shoulder. "My brave, brave April. Be proud of yourself for coming. I'm proud." Leaning forward, he kissed her cheek.

"You asked that I consider your words, and I've thought of nothing else. I've barely slept. I'm drawn to you, there is no doubt. Dr. Ashburn, Dewey, and even my own heart warns me that I'm trusting too soon. That I'll get hurt. Everyone worries I'll become sick again. But I am angry with them, Ryan." Frowning, she met his gaze. "They always say they want me to get better, that I need to face the real world, yet now that I am, they try to hold me back. I wish they would tell me I'll be all right, but they can't, can they?"

"No, baby, they can't." He squeezed her hand, which had a very tight grip on his shoulder.

"You can't tell me that either, can you?"

"No." But he should probably tell her about his agreement with her father. But it'd ruin her moment. *Yeah, go with that excuse, Cole. Good one.*

"I'm the only one who can make sure I'm all right. I've thought a lot about what that means. But, the answer was unclear until you showed me." She touched his face with her shaky hand as a single tear fell down her cheek. "You sat with a friend, and you told her a story you've told no one else. You opened your heart. You were brave enough, so I will be, too."

"Don't make me a hero, April, because I'm anything but." Throat tight, he wiped away her tear. "I have many faults." Number one being he'd lied to her from the very beginning.

"Too late." She gazed up at him through lowered lashes. "You're my hero in a to-go cup."

He laughed. "April, I believe you just made a joke."

She nodded, expression serious. "I can be quite funny, sometimes."

He pressed his lips together. "Right."

"I decided on the way over here I should like to see a movie. Isn't that what people do, who are, well…dating?"

Dating? What in the hell was he doing? Yet, the light in her eyes made him incapable of holding back. "Sure. Want to go now?"

"Oh, I don't even know what's playing. *Can* you go?"

"I'll grab Jones from the back." He pulled his cell phone from his pocket. "Let's check show times for this afternoon." After scrolling through the options, he stopped for a second and glanced over, studying April's bent head.

This moment was huge, not only in her life, but also in his. He'd been struck by the big C—commitment. What had she done to him? And what would he do if, like Dewey said, all the pieces fell before they had time to cement into place?

Mid-July gave him around a month and a half to discover the answers. And the first building block was taking his girl on a date.

CHAPTER 12

Two weeks later, while waiting for April to finish in his bathroom, Ryan sat on his couch and shifted his severely strained cock, locked tight in his jeans.

They'd been dating.

And he'd been patient. So patient, in fact, he figured the Catholics would show up at his door and crown him a saint, or whatever they did to people who performed miracles. Keeping his hands from straying all over April's perfect body *was* a miracle, especially when she was so eager to be touched.

In public, if too many people surrounded them, she'd shy away, but she was very comfortable kissing and snuggling. A fact for which he was grateful, but continually halting any further sexual activities was straining his nerves and his poor dick. Second base still seemed a long way off.

Although he'd had plenty of chances, he hadn't revealed his agreement with her father, and Senator David still touched base a couple times each week.

Tonight, he and April had gone to see their third movie and ended up back at his place. She was in the bathroom washing her hands. A habit he hadn't commented on—everyone had their quirks.

April came back and, with a joyful squeal, jumped on him

81

and began kissing his face before suddenly stopping. "You're whiskery tonight." She ran a hand up and down his cheek.

His cock instantly stiff, he shifted beneath her, breathing deeply of her faintly floral scent. "Is whiskery a word?"

"If it isn't, it should be." She heaved a sigh then settled back on her knees.

"What is it?" He rubbed at the worry lines forming between her brow.

"I was thinking of the movie." Her chest heaved with another long sigh beneath her short-sleeved blue top.

"Okay." He knew, if he waited long enough, she'd spill. He'd given up trying to read her mind. The complexities were too much for his mortal self. Maybe when he became a saint, he'd understand.

"Do you want to have sex?"

Whoa! Slow down, libido, she doesn't mean it. But his cock cried tears of joy and shouted, "Hell yes!"

"I need you to clarify." He tipped up her chin. "But the answer to that question is yes, with you, very much."

"I thought so." April squeezed her hands together, then jerked them apart and fisted them at her sides. "People in movies and on TV shows seem to like sex, and my therapist says, with the right person, the act is enjoyable."

"Yes." He would let this play out, he would not hope—or dream of sinking deep inside her body, of taking her for the first time, and making her his. He wouldn't consider that at all. Nope.

"My first experience with sex." She visibly swallowed, but continued. "Was horrific."

His heart dropped to his stomach and started thumping around with all the theatre popcorn and the twenty-four gallons of pop, making him queasy.

"When I was seven, I went with my mom to Africa."

Oh, holy fuck, did he really want to hear this? He ran his hands up and down her jean-clad thighs. "April, whatever you're about to say, it won't matter."

"It will matter. It *does* matter. You deserve to know. You told me about the puppy...now it's my turn."

"You sure?" He clutched her rigid fists in his hands.

"Yes, so you be quiet this time." She met his gaze, her blue eyes glistening with unshed tears. "I've never told another the entire story."

Ryan brought her hands to his lips and kissed them. "Then, I'm honored."

She leaned down and kissed his forehead. "Quiet, remember."

He nodded and mimed zipping his mouth shut.

April sat beside him on the couch, placing both hands in her lap. "While visiting Africa, mother and I were abducted from our car in the middle of a busy street. We were taken to a building that looked like it had been bombed. Crumbled concrete walls. Open ceilings. I was kept in a bathroom stall. My mother..." April heaved in a deep breath and huffed it back out. "My mother...was not with me. Each day, these young girls, teenagers really, they would bring me food, but I wouldn't eat it. They wouldn't speak to me. They were bruised, bloody. Their clothes were torn and dirty. A man came in one day, barely older than the girls." She paused a moment, her gaze locked on her clenched hands, distant, remembering. "He dragged me out of the stall by my hair, and he tried to do...things to me, but one of the girls came in and shouted at him. Then she flung off her clothes, and they...and they...they came together, making the most horrid of noises. But I knew what he was doing, and I knew she had taken my place. But I didn't know why."

Tears poured unheeded down her face. Her nose and chest turned a blotchy red.

"How old were you?"

"I told you. I was seven."

"I'm sorry. Right." Ryan cursed himself for not having any

tissues. "May I hold you?"

"No. Not until after." She reached over and took his hand. "I wondered why that girl would take my place. After he left, she remained on the floor, staring at the ceiling, and I realized the light in her eyes was gone. She was dead inside. I thought for a moment she was literally dead, until her gaze flicked toward mine. I leaned down, kissed her lips, and then held her." April brushed her fingers against her mouth. "I think I wanted to show her a kindness of some sort. I wrapped her in my arms, but she didn't return the embrace. I don't know how long we sat like that, but eventually she pulled away and left. I never saw her again."

April remained lost in her memories for a moment until she sneered. "That same young man came to check on me, and he brought in another girl. She was so young. I tried to stop him from hurting her, but he beat me back, smashing my head with the butt of his rifle. That's how I lost my hearing. I don't really remember much after that, but apparently two days later we were rescued."

In a soft voice, he said, "How long had you been there total?"

"Almost two months, at least that's what father says." Blinking away her tears, she looked at him and her entire body started to shake. "Excuse me." She shot off the couch and raced to the bathroom.

He could hear her retching. He'd known she'd seen and experienced horrendous things, but her story was real horror-film fodder. Revealing man at his worst. How would they overcome such a thing?

Practically hunched over, she snuck back in the room, eyes red-rimmed. "I'd like to go home now." She wiped her mouth with the back of her hand. Then, eyes wide, she lifted her hands and stared at them both. "I'm dirty."

"April, look at me." Standing, he snapped his fingers, gaining her attention. "I need to say something, and then I'll take you home."

She met his gaze, her chest heaving as if she fought to stop her heart from bursting out of her chest.

They'd just taken another huge step in their relationship, and they both needed time to adjust. He understood that. "I want to comfort you, but I realize my touch might be too much right now." He stepped toward her but stopped about two feet away. "What you saw was beyond anything I can comprehend. I'm grateful you trusted me with your story. I hope the telling eases some of the pain. I know I felt lighter after I told you about my...about Puppy."

Her dazed expression didn't change. "I need to go. My hands are dirty. I'm dirty."

Yikes. The phobia had kicked in and taken over. He understood why it would rise to the surface now. After he walked her home, he'd call Dewey and give him a heads up. "All right. Okay. You've had enough for one night." He slipped on his shoes and led her out the door. "Let's get you home." On the walk to her townhouse, he didn't touch her or say another word.

Because sometimes silence *was* golden.

CHAPTER 13

Now that the crazy evening at Galaxy was almost over, he sang along with an old hip-hop tune and pulled chilled beer bottles from their cardboard box, stacking them in the cooler.

After their Monday night movie date, Ryan didn't see April Tuesday or Thursday. He worked at the bar on Friday night, and took a shift at the Jiffy Oil Saturday, then slogged through hours at the bar again tonight. He'd texted April a few times, and on Friday she'd responded that she was working through some things and would come see him soon.

His tip jar was a little light, due to his surly behavior, which was because of the blonde currently walking up to the bar. *What the hell?*

"What are you doing here?" He glanced at the Budweiser clock on the wall. "It's after one. Where's Dewey?"

April smiled at him as though she hadn't been incommunicado all week. Her light blue T-shirt matched her eyes and her hands were buried in her jeans' front pockets. "I used a driver app, Ryan. I *am* capable of doing things by myself."

He shoved another bottle into the cooler. "Dewey isn't with you?"

"No." She stepped to the side when a tall brunette pressed in beside her and slurred her request for a Malibu rum and pineapple juice.

Ryan gritted his teeth. "Just a second." He held up a finger at the brunette and kept his gaze locked on the blonde. "April, do you realize what Dewey's going to do...no...what he'll do *to me* when he finds out you're gone?"

"I have to do things on my own Ryan."

"You tell him, sister." The brunette raised her hand for a high-five.

April looked at the woman's hand then finally lifted her own and awkwardly patted it. "Yes. Yes, I'll tell him!"

"Okay. Enough with the female bonding." Rolling his eyes, he rested his chilled fingers on his hips. She did need to become independent. Wasn't that the whole point of this exercise? He should be praising her, but some part of him, buried not as far down as he believed, wasn't quite ready to share her with the rest of the world.

"Can I get my drink?" The brunette tapped her credit card against the bar.

Obviously, the rest of the world wouldn't wait. "April, would you like a drink?"

She looked at the brunette. "Excuse me. What was your drink order?"

"Malibu rum and pineapple juice."

April nodded. "Right. I'll have one of those, as well."

"Fine." He flipped two glasses up on the counter but made sure April's had a bit more juice than rum.

# # #

Ryan lifted his damp Metallica T-shirt over his head. "April, listen, you can't spend the night here. Dewey will roast my nuts if he finds out."

She grinned. "That's funny."

"Oh?" He tossed his shirt at the hamper. "I'm glad you find burnt nuts amusing."

She stood and walked over to him then placed her hands upon his chest. "You said you wanted to have...um...sex. I would like to try."

Ryan's heart rate shot through the roof, and his cock stood up and said, "Ready for lift off." But no. Maybe no. He really should say, no.

But she was tracing her fingers across his abs. And her breathing was harsh and her cheeks flushed. His cock might just shoot off the landing pad without his countdown. "April." He gently placed his hand over hers and pressed it against his heart. "Feel that? That's fear. Something I've never felt with a woman before...but you scare the shit out of me."

She chuckled. "You have nothing on fear. Fear is my life, but because of you, because I want to change, I'm here. Touching you lights up my whole body. I don't touch people, Ryan. I don't like even speaking to people. I don't know why, but with you...doing so is effortless. Well, no, that's a lie." She stepped back and waved a hand at the couch. "Could we sit a moment? I'd like to explain why I've come to this decision."

She took his hand and led him to the couch, sat, then shot back up again and paced in front of him. "When I left your place the other night, after I'd told you my story, I went home and showered." She bit her lip and met his gaze. "Not showered like a normal person, but for an hour in steaming hot water. And...it wasn't the first time. Every time I leave you, every time someone touches me, I go home and wash it off. And I hate it!" Her hands clenched into fists at her sides. "I hate who I am. I hate that I'm afraid of everything. That I need all these drugs to help me through the day. But I hurt the most when I wash away you." Lower lip wobbling, she crumpled to her knees before him, took his hand, and pressed it against her cheek. "I need to stay. To touch you. I want that connection, and I want to be strong enough to keep your scent on my skin. Sometimes, I can still smell you when I leave, and I don't even know how to describe the scent other than, it's just you. Then, when it's gone, I hate myself."

Though shocking, he needed to understand this side of her. The side that scared him. The side he couldn't understand or change. "April, it's okay."

"No!" She shook her head, her blonde hair whipping back and forth on her shoulders. "It's not okay. *I'm* not okay. You don't know me." She shifted up and perched her butt on the coffee table, her gaze on her feet. "I'm afraid of germs. Afraid to touch people. Afraid of basically everything, but this week, I've come to understand that the one thing I'm really afraid of…is losing you. So, I want to try. I want to be different. I want to be like that girl at the bar tonight. Sexy and confident. And just enjoying normal things."

Ryan swallowed the lump in his throat. "I'm proud of you. You've come really far. Look at you. You're here now. And if you need to shower or leave, if at any time our relationship is ever too much, then just tell me." He slipped her hair over her ear. "Did these phobias start because of your captivity?"

"I've always been quiet, and a lot shy. I'd rather escape into a book than talk to people. When I came back from Africa, I was so afraid of everything. I jumped at shadows, mostly because I could no longer hear. Silence can be frightening." She shivered. "Then…I lost my mother, and I completely stopped speaking, stopped eating, stopped living…for three years. Father didn't know what to do with me, so he sent me to a private facility where I just survived for a while. I hadn't adjusted to my hearing loss, was traumatized by what I'd seen while imprisoned, my mother left me, and so…I broke. I stayed broken for almost eight years. Didn't emerge until I was eighteen." She sniffed. "I think the more I locked myself away, the more afraid I became to emerge."

"Makes sense." But eight years at a private facility. What did that do to a person? Hell, she was only twenty-one now. "Maybe I should take you home, give you more time."

"No." Her blue eyes blazed. "I came here to be with you. I shouldn't have told you all that information. Now you think I'm even weirder." Her shoulders slumped. "I've ruined everything."

"Hey. Stop that. No sad face." Ryan tipped up her chin. "April, we don't have to jump right in to touching. We can continue with holding hands and soft kisses. Sex can wait." He shifted as he heard his balls groan in dismay. They were beyond blue now and had likely turned into some horrid violet shade.

"But, Ryan, I have to try. I'll be brave, and we'll see how I do." She pulled her shirt over her head.

No bra. Oh, holy shit. Perfection. Her breasts had to be like a C-cup. And the tips were a perfect pink, blush rose. "Whoa." Ryan held up a hand. "Why? What?" His dick sent him a mental message, *Dude, you're freaking out. Get your head out of your ass.* Ryan shook his head. "You're not...you're not wearing a bra."

"No. I thought you would like to see me this way."

"I do. I like it. Yeah." His hand lifted, as if moving to touch her without his consent, so he forced it back down. "I'm sorry. I'm stunned."

"Why? You've been with women before, and I want you to think of me that way. You said you did." April's brow furrowed and she glanced at her shirt on the floor. "Should I put my shirt back on?"

"No!" Leaning forward, Ryan braced a hand on her shoulder. "No. Let me catch my breath. You are so beautiful." He massaged her neck. "Is this okay?"

Her lids lowered. "Yes. I feel all floaty."

He grinned. "Floaty is good." He could do this. Introduce her to intimacy. He could play naughty professor. That'd work. He undid the button on his jeans, giving his erection a little wiggle room. "I'm going to touch your breast now."

April heaved in a deep breath and squeezed her eyes shut.

"All right."

He trailed a finger down her neck and ran it along the top of her right breast.

She shivered and then gasped. "That's very nice. You can do more, if you'd like." She opened her eyes. "May I touch you, too?"

"Sure." He swallowed.

She dropped on her knees between his legs and ran her hands up his thighs. "I watched videos this week. Maria told me what to search for on the computer."

"Oh, yeah." His voice turned husky. Just thinking of her watching porn had him picturing her in all kinds of positions—on his bed, over his couch. "What did you see?"

"Well...I saw everything." She glanced at him before running her hands up his chest. "Their faces would get all scrunched up, but then they'd shout and seemed to enjoy themselves at the end."

"The end *is* enjoyable."

She nodded and bit her bottom lip. "I'd like to know."

A vivid image of April in the throes of climax flashed through his mind. All pink skin, wet lips, heaving chest. Ryan groaned. "I'm not sure—"

Standing, April pressed a finger against his lips. "I'm here because I want to know."

He held her gaze for a moment. "You do this, you'll stay with me. In my bed, in my arms. No fear. You can shower if you need to, but you'll have to accept me during. Germs and all."

"I think I'll like your germs." She quirked a grin then settled on his lap again.

He wrapped a hand around the back of her neck. "I'm kissing you now."

"Okay." She whispered against his lips.

He pressed his lips against hers then ran his tongue along the seam of her mouth until she opened with a soft gasp. The light puff of air brushed against his lips, the scent of pineapple and rum clouding his senses. He kept the kiss light, toying with her tongue.

She groaned and then trailed her fingertips down his chest. Easing back, she stood and unzipped her jeans.

Pale white legs of untouched skin emerged. Her panties were plain white cotton. He inwardly grinned. That was his April. "This is a big leap, April." Why would he do this when she'd taken a whole week to come to him? Moving forward with their relationship *would* help him solidify their connection. Yet, he wasn't quite sure this was such a great idea. They wouldn't have sex, but he could show her pleasure. Decision made, he ran a finger along the waistband of her underwear.

Eyes wide, she watched his finger. "I like when you touch me. I shiver all over, and my heart starts pounding. I can do this. Please, take them off."

He drew his gaze up her body until he met those light-blue eyes. "Hmmm...I want them off, too, but you need to tell what's okay and what isn't." He stood and pressed her down onto the couch. "Lie here."

She settled beneath him, resting her arms across her full breasts.

"Let me look at you."

April hesitated then placed her arms at her sides. "Okay. Do you think I'm pretty?"

"No. Not pretty. Not even close." With a finger, he rubbed away the frown lines between her brows. "You are my dream. My everything." As he said the words, he realized how true they were. Realized in such a short time, he didn't want to live without her. With her body laid out before him, everything became clear. Became easy. She was his. End of story. He'd suffered through his life and so had she. Their relationship was meant from the beginning. They completed each other in ways no one would ever understand. So, he'd savor her trust and her first foray into pleasure.

He bent and took her peaked nipple into his mouth.

She yelped and bent her knees, arching her entire body

toward him. "Oh...oh, that's why they...I-I want more. Please, don't stop."

With one hand caressing her belly, he gave one final tug on her nipple before he kissed his way to her lips.

She opened eagerly, unschooled but following his lead.

Sensations he'd never felt before shot through his body. A foreign emotion washed over him. Who knew genuine affection would make every kiss, every brush of her tongue so much...more.

"Touch me. Underneath," she gasped against his mouth.

He growled then delved deep again, kissing her until he couldn't breathe, all while he trailed his fingers along her inner thighs and over her slight mound.

Breaking the kiss, he tugged her nipple into his mouth at the same time he worked his hand under her panties. "This okay?"

"Mmmhmm." April lifted her head and stared down her body. "I'm so wet."

He shuddered as he eased his finger through her folds. "Yeah, you are." He kissed her shoulder. "Wet for me. I want to slide inside you. Make you mine...but not tonight. Tonight is all about you."

Her hips lifted, and he swore he'd never seen anything so beautiful. Her chest pink, her lips wet and slightly red, her eyes watching his hand move against her body. But the visual wasn't complete. Sliding his finger against her clit, he pulled free.

She gasped and turned to him. "No."

He loosened the zipper on his jeans.

"Oh, should I?" She sat up on her elbows. "Should I touch you, too?"

He pressed a quick kiss against her lips. "No. I'm good."

"But I want to see you."

"Holy hell, April. You're killing me."

She grinned. "I know."

"Ah, someone's a little cheeky." He pulled his cock free of

his boxer briefs. "There. Say hello, ya big dick, 'cause that's all you get tonight."

April touched his cock head then ran her finger across his dripping slit. "Seeing your penis makes me feel...I want to know what it would feel like inside me. I want you inside me."

Ryan groaned and dropped his head on her chest. "April, I can't do that. Not tonight."

"Why?" April's voice cracked. "I want to try."

He lifted his head. "I won't rush this. I want to enjoy each step."

"But, your penis is purple. Does it hurt?" She ran her fingers through his happy trail before circling his dripping tip.

"I'll be honest. Yes, it does, but you can watch me touch myself as I touch you. Will that be okay?"

"Yes." She nodded. "I want you to have an orgasm if I have one."

"We can do that, but I want to take off your panties first. Can I do that?"

"Yes." Lifting her hips, she wiggled out of her underwear then folded them and placed them on the floor.

Squeezing the head of his dick with his left hand, he let his right drift over her mound of light-brown pubic hair. "April, look at me. I want you to only see me. Nothing else. Think about no one else. These moments are ours. No phobias. No past fears. Just you and me. Can you do that? Can you be with just me?"

"I am with you." Breathing ragged, she lifted her hips again. "I trust you to make me feel good."

He slid his fingers over her wet folds and pressed against her nub.

"Yes, I like that."

Oh, fuck, so did he. Keeping his gaze on hers, he ran his hand up and down his thick erection. While sliding his other hand over her mound, pressing against her with his palm, he eased a finger inside her core.

"Ryan, yes. That feels so nice. Please, push harder." April rocked her hips in time with the thrusting of his finger. Then she dropped her gaze to his hand. "I'm watching."

"Ah, April. That's so hot." Spitting in his hand, he worked his cock even faster. Her words had lit a fire in his body that burned down his spine and detonated in his balls. He slipped another finger into her wet core and pressed against her slick folds.

She gasped, and her neck arched. "I think I'm coming, Ryan. I can feel it."

So could he. Her slick channel tightened around his fingers then her hips arched, and she cried out as she came. No filter. Pure pleasure revealed in each gasp and moan. He'd never seen anything more erotic.

He held back his own orgasm for a second, but seeing her release, watching her body twitch with each wave, tipped him over. Hot streams of cum poured out his cock, coating his hand in warmth. The smell of their combined pleasure filled the air, and he greedily breathed it in.

She turned and met his gaze.

That was all it took for his dick to shudder again. That heated look was too much. He hissed out a breath as he slowed his movements, both on himself and inside her core.

April hummed out a sigh then ran her fingers over his cum-covered hand. "It's slick."

"Yes." If she expected him to form sentences, she was out of her mind. He'd never come so hard in his life. His cock was still twitching in his hand.

"Can we do that again?"

A joyous sound erupted from his chest then he burst out laughing. Hell yes, they could do that again. He'd likely lose his mind, but he'd do whatever he had to—for April.

"Why are you laughing?" Brow furrowed, she tugged on his hair.

He met her slightly hooded gaze. "Nothing but pure joy, baby. Pure joy. Now, let's see if you can rest beside me in your birthday suit."

"I can."

Could she? He considered her phobias. Maybe they should get cleaned up a little. "I'm going to wash up." He jerked his head toward his cum-covered hand. "Do you need to shower?"

"You won't mind?"

"No. I'm trying to understand what you need, and if you want to shower, then be my guest." He pulled her up and led her to the bathroom closet. "Here." He opened the door and pulled out a towel and washcloth. "Go on. I'll wash my hands in the kitchen."

She took the towel and then lifted up on her tippy-toes and kissed his cheek. "Thank you, Ryan."

He waited until she entered the bathroom and shut the door before leaning his forearm against his wall and taking a deep breath. This befriend-April scheme had not gone as planned. They were so much more than friends, which meant he had to tell her the truth about how they'd met.

On the other side of the door, April belted out some country song while in the shower. A happy sound. Carefree and splendid. He wouldn't ruin her joy.

The secret could wait.

CHAPTER 14

The next morning, Ryan jolted awake to his phone chiming with the senator's ring tone. Not that April would know the sound was assigned to her father, but still. He glanced over at the blonde mass of hair spread across his pillow.

She hadn't stirred.

He patted his hand against the side table, feeling for his phone. He'd placed it there last night after April had fallen asleep and he was waiting for Dewey to call—or storm down his door. Blinking awake, he pressed the Talk button. "Yeah?"

"Cole." The senator's voice came across the line. "Is April still with you?"

"Yeah." Was he in trouble because she'd stayed? Of course, they knew where she was 24/7. He prepared a mental argument as the subject of said discussion popped up with her halo of rumpled bed-head and met his gaze.

"Who is it?" she mumbled, rubbing her eyes.

"Work." True...in a sense. Ryan rolled out of bed. "Give me a minute." Heading for the bathroom, he shut the door and whispered, "Why are you calling? April's fine."

"The press has found out. How, I don't know, but the story is out."

"What story?" Why should the press care that April had

97

spent the night in his apartment? He yelped when his bare ass hit the cold edge of the sink.

The senator sighed heavily. "April isn't really my daughter."

"What?" This time, his tone was much louder and very shocked, confused, and... *What!?*

"April was already one year old when I met Anna. My wife had a previous boyfriend who'd hoped to gain entrance into her world. Anna's father figured out his scheme, paid him off, and had him agree he'd never bother them again. The thing is...April doesn't know."

Not good. She was doing so well, too. He could hear her humming some tune just on the other side of the door. Would this news push her over the edge? How unstable was she? He stared at himself in the mirror. Was he qualified to help her get through something this insane or should he call Dr. Ashburn?

"A rather large, and rather loud, group of reporters are outside my office and the townhouse. I plan on giving a statement later, and the picture would be better if April was by my side."

Ryan stared at the phone as if it'd turned into a foreign object. What had the senator just said? He wanted April to stand in front of a bunch of reporters? "No, no, and hell no. What are you thinking? You can't tell her you aren't her father then expect her to stand calmly by your side while you answer a thousand questions she doesn't know the answers to. What's the matter with you?"

"I'm sending Dewey over. I need you to come back with them."

Ryan stared at the bathroom door, considering the woman on the other side. Had the senator done that? Considered April? "This is a horrible idea."

"Yes, but this needs to be done before she hears the truth another way."

"You just said reporters are waiting outside. She'll hear it then. They'll bombard her with questions."

"Well, I suggest...I'd like you to tell her. Get her ready, Ryan. An Ivy league education isn't cheap." And then he hung up.

Fucking hung up.

On the verge of throwing his phone against the wall, he stopped when April appeared in the doorway. Naked. She had no concept of self-consciousness. His dick grew thick just thinking about how free she was, unencumbered by all the negativity most women felt about their bodies. Guess that's what came from having good genes. Though, thinking about her genes, combined with the news he'd just heard, had him seriously disoriented. And before coffee, too. *That* was unconscionable.

"What is wrong?" April held her hands together at her waist. "Do you need to leave?"

Hell yes, he needed to leave. Actually, they both did. Screw what her dad wanted. No, they couldn't run from this. "That was your father."

April took a small step back, brushing her hair off her shoulder. "Why is he calling you? Is he angry I'm here? I don't care, Ryan. It's my choice. He wanted me out, so I'm out, and he can't say a word. I will have you if I want. I'm old enough to make my own decisions."

"Whoa! It's okay." Her fiery tirade was doing wonders for his libido. But they didn't have time for such things. "He's not concerned with that. Dewey gave him my number." Ryan avoided her gaze and wrapped her in his arms. *Naked!* He couldn't tell her distressing news with her naked, and him naked, and legs, and arms, and soft skin. God, she smelled good. "Okay." He eased away slowly. "I need you dressed, before I lose my mind. Let's go back to the bedroom."

"All right." Though she frowned, she followed him over to the bed.

Seeing her sitting on top of his covers, all long limbs and creamy skin, he cursed as he fought off the urge to press her onto her back and climb between her legs. He couldn't take her to the pinnacle of pleasure one moment, and then in the next break her heart with her father's revelation. His dick tried to argue that fact, so Ryan shoved on his jeans and mentally shouted at the fucker to calm its shit down. He had to tell April what was happening before Dewey arrived. He nudged her farther up the bed, settled on top of her, and then kissed her softly. So, yeah, he could do this with her naked.

She widened her knees and wrapped her arms around his neck.

On a groan, he unwrapped her arms, and placed them together across her bare chest. A man could only deal with so much temptation, after all. "April, I need to tell you something." How was this fair? He never wanted to break her heart, but now he had no choice. How should he explain? Usually, he'd just blurt out the truth. He couldn't do that, but was there any other way?

"It's bad, isn't it?" April's hair rustled against his pillow as she tilted her head.

Seven thousand curses raged in his head for her pain in the ass father. "A secret's been revealed, and yeah, it's gonna hurt. But *do not* internalize your feelings. I want to know how you feel. Do *not* shut me out. What happened last night meant the world to me, so don't hurt me by blocking me out. We're together now, remember?"

"I remember." A tear trickled down her cheek. "Did my father yell at you? Are you leaving me?"

"No." Her worry was so sweet and he wanted some of her sugar so he bent and brushed a quick kiss on her lips. "That's not it, at all. I could eat you up, but...another time."

"I would be very hurt if you left." She sighed then ran her finger along his jaw. "I'm sorry to burden you with that information, but you have asked for honesty."

"You aren't a burden." How could he get through this moment with his heart beating outside of his chest...hell, the damn thing was in her hands. She had the power to break him, now. But first, they had to get past him breaking her.

"I don't care what my father thinks. I'm not going home yet." Her tone was pure stubborn and her hands strayed across his bare chest and down.

"April, honey, I need you to listen." Ryan stopped her hand from taking a trip through his happy trail. "This is about your father, and yes, about you, too."

"Is he all right?"

"April." He pressed his forehead against hers then sat back on his knees. "Do not ask questions until I finish." He sighed as he realized he was taking out his frustrations on her. "I don't even know how to say this…and I'm super-pissed I'm the one having to hurt you."

Her lower lip jutted out. "I'm sorry."

"No, don't be. I'm messing this up. You've done nothing wrong." He took a deep breath. He couldn't show sympathy. He needed her strong. "All right, I'm going to spit it out. A reporter did some digging. Apparently, you were already a year old when your mother met your father. Do you understand? Your father isn't your biological father."

April was quiet then her lower lip wobbled. "May I sit up, please?"

"April, stay with me here. He still raised you. He's still your father."

"I would like to be alone for a few minutes." Her entire body stiffened, and she rubbed her hands together. The happy gleam in her eyes now gone.

"April, stop. You do that hand thing every time you're upset." He took her hands and held them on each side of her head. "Don't break on me."

"I need you to leave, please." She closed her eyes.

"I can't." His heart jumped to his throat, and for some stupid reason, he felt like crying—a common occurrence around this woman.

She tugged free of his grip, covered her face with her hands, and burst into tears, her entire body quaking. A horrid keening sound pouring from her lips.

He barely heard the knock on his door over her heart-wrenching sobs. "Damn it. I don't know what to do for you." She'd curled up onto her side, so he leaned down and kissed her cheek. "I'll give you a second, but I'll be right back. That's probably Dewey."

After throwing on a T-shirt, he stomped over to the door and opened it, hoping Dewey got in his face, because he needed an outlet for all this aggression.

Dewey barged in. "Where is she?" The big guy took off for the bedroom.

"Wait a damn minute…" Ryan grabbed his arm and whipped him around.

Dewey cursed and swung his right fist.

Ryan ducked then stepped out of reach. "Stop it. She doesn't need you going all ape-man right now. Plus, she's not dressed. Not only that, I'm itching for a fight. So back off right now!"

"I can hear her crying. What did you do?"

"What did *I* do? You and your Senator are the ones making her cry, because you've kept this secret her whole life." Ryan placed a hand against his pounding head, remembering April was upset and shouldn't be yelling at Dewey. Not only that, this much stress before coffee was entirely uncalled for. "You're not going in there until she is dressed and calm."

Ryan didn't know what kind of shit Dewey had dealt with when handling April in the past, but she was his woman now, and he'd be the only one seeing her bare—both emotionally and physically.

"She needs to come home. I know this news is insane…and I'm sorry, okay? I'm just as pissed as you are." Dewey chewed on his thumbnail. Shifting in his jeans and white dress shirt that was buttoned completely wrong, as if he'd thrown it on and headed over. "How is she?"

"You have ears, as you said, she's upset. I need to get back in there. Wait here. We'll come out when she's ready. I don't care about Senator David's stupid-ass news conference."

Dewey nodded then waved a hand at the door. "Reporters followed me here."

"Then leave."

"I can't. She's…I'm worried. I won't let her face those cameras alone."

"Then grab a beer, watch some TV, and I'll call if I need you."

CHAPTER 15

After twenty minutes of soothing, April finally quieted.

She had a death grip on his shoulders, and his shirt was damp from her tears. Ryan rocked her back and forth, whispering platitudes, curses, anything to let her know she was perfectly justified in her outburst.

"I have something I've never told you." She sniffed, eased out of his arms, and settled against his headboard.

"Listen, you don't have to say anything right now." With his thumb, he rubbed between her eyebrows before kissing the tip of her blotchy nose.

"No, I must explain, and then I promise I'll be strong again."

"I'll be strong for you." He brushed her tear-drenched hair from the side of her face.

"I've let that happen for too long. I need to get better, and I need to tell you this. Something I've never told another." She heaved in a deep breath then glanced at him through wet lashes. "It's likely I love you. Isn't that what love is, trusting someone with your very soul? My soul was broken a long time ago, as was my heart, but with you, I want them to heal. I want to be a bird, soaring free from its cage. And in order to fly high, I have to tell this story to someone, and I want it to be you."

"Before you start, let me get you some tissues first." He

stopped by the bathroom door. "Dewey's out in the living room, so maybe get dressed, all right?"

She nodded.

In the bathroom, he took a deep breath. Seeing her break like that had been intense. He grabbed a new toilet paper roll and headed back into the bedroom.

She took it but frowned. "This isn't tissue."

"It's man-tissue."

After blowing her nose, she patted the bed at her side. "My mother already told me about my father."

"She did?"

"Yes, but I never believed her because when she told me..." April bit her lip before breathing deep. "She told me the day she killed herself."

He glanced at the door, and then grabbed his phone to check the time. "April, we don't have to do this today. We can just stay here in our cocoon." Ryan lifted her chin with his index finger and stared into her blue depths.

"I do." She eased his finger from her face and wrapped her hand in his. "After our abduction, we were both damaged in so many ways. Still, we were the only ones who understood what happened. We needed each other, but lately she had been crying more. Told me she worried about my future, about who I would become. She said we were both damaged.

"Because of her words, I took to wearing layers of clothing, embarrassed about something but not quite sure what. She stopped speaking to me. Stopped spending time with me. I felt I had done something wrong. I wrote her letters, asking her the questions only little girls have. I was so frightened all the time. She was my lifeline, and she'd abandoned me." April fiddled with the bath tissue, ripping it into tiny pieces. "One morning, she came to see me." April cleared her throat and flicked two fingers by her cheek. "They had scarred her face and body, but I didn't see the marks, I only saw her. She wanted to take a drive and have a picnic. I was so excited to spend time with her again. She told me to gather all the things I loved most and that we would leave at four. Mother was the thing I loved most, but I wanted to be dutiful, so I packed."

Not wanting to interrupt by speaking, Ryan grabbed her used tissue, tossed it to the floor, rolled off another, and handed it over.

"Oh, thanks." April smiled. "So, my mom came right at four, and we left. She was singing along with the radio and talking a mile a minute during the commercials. We drove and drove until she ended up in southern Indiana. We got out and had our picnic but it was very dark. She didn't eat anything, but made sure I did. All my favorites—fried chicken, mac and cheese, vanilla cake with pink icing. And a root beer. She rarely let me eat like this, so I was excited about the treat. Then she started talking about how no one would love us, and we only had each other. She said we were damaged and ugly and that Father no longer wanted us, and we had to move on. Then she laughed and said he wasn't even my real father, so he didn't matter. She told me she would make everything right, that we wouldn't suffer anymore. Then she held me, kissed the top of my head, and said we would be together forever." April sighed then took a deep breath. "She smelled like roses."

Ryan wrapped her against him, aching for the little girl who'd endured so much. Offering comfort, he smoothed his hand up and down her chilled arm. "You smell like roses, too." Only she could have him talking of something as frou-frou as flowers. He refrained from rolling his eyes.

"I'm not finished." April settled at his side, her head resting on his shoulder. "I watched her take a handful of pills. We were both under lots of medication at the time, so I didn't think anything of it. She left all the picnic stuff at the table and had me get into the car. I didn't want to leave any trash behind, but she was in a hurry.

"Once in the car, she told me not to put on my seatbelt. I

thought that was odd, since normally I was expected to do that. Then she turned up the radio and took off, fast. You know most forest roads are really curvy, right?"

He nodded.

"Well, she took the turns at reckless speeds. I got scared and secretly fastened my seatbelt. About five miles away from our picnic, she lost control, and we slammed head first into a tree." April took a breath as she ripped through that part, talking fast as if trying to get through the whole story quickly.

"After I don't even know how much time passed, I woke with a horrible pain across my body and saw my mother on the hood of the car. The engine was smoking, and we were really close to the tree. Blood was everywhere. After everything I'd been through, seeing all that red pour from her body was what pushed me over the edge. I disappeared into some deep part of myself and didn't return for a few years. She was right when she said I was damaged. I am. But so are a lot of other people." April traced circles on his thigh with her index finger, pausing for a moment. "I have to live. I can't only see red. I have to see everything. I want to see the color of your skin. Your brown eyes. Your colorful tattoos. Everything."

"And you have and will." He held her tighter against his side. "Thank you for telling me that story. I'm sorry about your mom."

"I'm sorry, too. I think I died that day, as well. Or, at least, I let myself drown in darkness, but I don't want to do that anymore. As a matter of fact, after I go speak to my father, I want you to take me to get a tattoo. I want color on my body."

Hmm, well…tears and tattoos shouldn't mix. "Right now might not be the best time to make a decision about something so permanent. Plus, your father wants you to stand at his side during a press conference." Ryan kissed the top of her head. "I don't know that you'll be up for a tattoo after being around all those people."

"If I know you're there, I'll be okay. I'll just stand quietly, think about you, and draw out a tattoo in my mind."

Though unsure of this tattoo idea, after all, ink *was* permanent, he'd placate her for now. "Sure. Whatever you need to do. Dewey and I will protect you. All right?"

April nodded and kissed his cheek. "May I take another shower now?"

He bent and kissed her, long, soft, and gentle with a light brush of his tongue against hers. At the edge of wanting to take the kiss deeper, he eased back. "What I want is to join you in the shower, but instead, I'll sketch some tattoo ideas, all right?"

"I can shower by myself, Ryan." April furrowed her brow then her cheeks turned pink. "Oh…I see. You wanted to touch me in the shower, didn't you?"

"Yes. Just thinking about all that water rolling down your skin." He shivered dramatically. "Damn."

"I don't know that I'm ready for that yet. I kind of…My showers are sort of a place I go to…I can't explain what I mean." She cupped his cheek. "I'm sorry."

"You don't have to explain. I understand." He kissed her with a hard smack of his lips. "Get up and shower, stinky."

She laughed and shifted her legs to the side of the bed. "You make me happy."

He grinned. With those words, she squeezed his heart in her hand. She did a hell of a lot more than make him laugh. Clearing his throat, he pressed against his cock, hardening in his jeans. "What kind of tattoo do you want?"

Her shoulders rose and fell with two deep breaths before she spoke in her usual loud tone, "I want a bird escaping a cage."

He could do that. He really could. He'd aid in her escape, yet he couldn't help but wonder if he'd be taking her place inside that cage, and she alone held the key.

CHAPTER 16

After the somewhat dicey news conference, April became an overnight sensation. All the news agencies spent hours reconstructing Senator David's and April's lives. Her beauty and her tragedy all added up to one juicy headline.

A reporter even tried to dig info from Ryan while sitting at the bar last night. He'd come in as a customer but left with a kick in the ass.

Ryan couldn't wait until the next big story came along so they'd leave her alone. Three days after the press conference, Ryan headed to April's place with a to-go cup of Earl Grey in his hand.

One good thing to come of this mess was April had actually sat down with her father and explained what happened the day of her mother's death.

The senator was sticking close and helping her through this time. His girlfriend, Cheri, was kind to April, as well.

Ryan would get her alone today, no matter what. Too many days had passed since he'd had her in his arms. They were leaving, one-way or another.

She was no longer a tragic figure, trying to escape her past. Her tattoo, a colorful robin flying free from the confines of a thorny cage, was testament to her new purpose. He'd made a midnight appointment with his favorite artist and held April's hand while the man drew out the whole piece on the back of her left shoulder.

She'd cried when it was complete.

And he'd admit to wiping away a tear of his own as he'd held her in his arms and told her over and over what a strong and brave woman she'd become.

Too bad he wasn't so brave himself, but he couldn't rip up her world with the truth about his agreement with her father when her life was in such turmoil. And that sounded like a pretty lame excuse, probably because it was.

# # #

Upon arriving at the townhouse, the senator cornered Ryan and led him into his home office.

Ryan hoped their visit wouldn't last much longer, or April's tea would get cold. Still, he settled into the leather chair and waited to hear what the man had to say, suffering through the usual pleasantries first.

"Thank you for how you've eased my daughter's worries since the news story broke. I hate that she's become some kind of celebrity. She doesn't understand the attraction of her beauty."

Since that was an understatement, and a sore point, he steered clear of that subject and said what had been on his mind throughout this whole ordeal. "I'd think you love all the attention, *Senator.*"

"You'd be wrong." David tapped his cell phone against his mahogany desk. "I have to play the game, though. Can't let them know anything's amiss, or they'll keep digging."

"Nothing left to find." Ryan shrugged. "Listen, I think we should tell April the truth about our agreement. This thing with her…she's come to mean a lot to me. I love her."

The tapping stopped. The father, not the senator glared for a moment. "Do you?"

"I do." Not that he'd told her yet. She'd basically said the words. He hadn't. But soon. Very soon.

"Loving her is easy. She's so much like her mother." David stared out the window into the humid August day.

"When you talk about Anna, that's the only time you seem real." Ryan studied the faraway look in the man's eye. That was love. Real and lasting. The kind that carried your thoughts to another place, and a happier time.

"April's mother took the best of me with her. All I have left is determination. Although, I must say, I now have hope for April, and that's what I wished to speak to you about." He rounded the desk and sat on the edge, sipping from his black "Vote David" coffee mug before continuing. "I spoke to a colleague at Harvard about you. He did some investigating and discovered you've been accepted."

What? Accepted? Ryan struggled to breathe. If he stood right now, he'd likely crumple to his knees and thank whatever gods had deemed him worthy enough to enter the hallowed halls of Harvard. And yet, what was he leaving behind? "I haven't received any info, and the semester starts in like two weeks."

"You were a last-minute addition." The senator winked.

Leaving his suspicions behind for a moment, he spoke from his heart—a heart currently pounding with far too many emotions. "What about April?"

"Yes, what about her?" David arched a blond brow.

"She'll come with me, of course." Ryan nodded while creating a mental bullet list of the reasons she should and would join him.

"I don't know if that's such a good plan. Maybe you should give her a couple semesters to get used to the idea of leaving. She's been through a lot recently. I don't want to push her too hard."

Ryan fisted both hands against his knees. Where had the

summer gone? He agreed with the senator, she needed more time. But they didn't have it. Not now. Not with all his dreams for the future opening before him. Yet, was April willing to go on this venture? Could he leave without her? Likely not. So, he'd work on an angle. A way to get her to agree. She'd broken free from her cage, but how far was she willing to fly?

The senator breezed over to his coffee maker and plopped another pod into the machine. "However, if you want to discuss the matter with April, you can let me know in a few days so my assistant can funnel money into your account. My daughter is used to living in a certain manner. I won't have her in some hovel or in an unsecure location."

Ryan stuck his tongue in his cheek before he railed at the senator for not believing he could support a woman. He wanted the best for April, as well, but a man had his limits. "I don't feel comfortable taking your money anymore, sir. I can look into financial aid, and as far as living expenses, I will take care of her."

"By what, Cole? Working two jobs and going to school at same time? I don't think so." The senator faced him with narrowed eyes. "Regardless of any DNA, April *is* my daughter, and *we* had an agreement. You'll get an education and support her in a proper manner. Her mother would want this, so don't argue. What's done is done."

Ryan clenched his jaw but agreed. He couldn't care for April if he was never home. He'd accept the assistance for her and her alone, but only until she was settled. Then he'd get a job. He nodded at the man then got up from his seat and stormed off to find his woman.

CHAPTER 17

Drumming his fingers on his kitchen table, Ryan studied the blonde sitting across from him. She'd barely touched her salad but had eaten the chicken and vegetables. He'd taken the weekend off in order to spend time with her. They'd escaped her father's townhouse, making a game of dodging reporters.

His knee bounced under the table, and he cursed the appendage as if it was a separate entity. How would he ever convince her of the merits of his plan? Plus, this was basically akin to a marriage proposal. Hell, maybe it should be. "Are you finished, April?"

When she nodded, he stood and tugged her over to the couch.

"Dinner was really wonderful. Thank you." She rubbed her flat belly. "I am happy we escaped. I hate all the attention, and I've missed coming to tea."

"I've missed you, too." Ryan eased an arm around her shoulders and pulled her onto his lap. "I want to discuss something with you." He briskly rubbed her arm, more to ease his own nerves than hers.

Keep moving. Keep talking, Don't wuss out.

"All right." She smiled and kissed his cheek.

As always, he tore right in. "Harvard accepted my

application."

She straightened and placed a hand over her wide-open mouth. "Oh my goodness."

He nodded, waiting for her to elaborate. Or cry. Or do something…he wasn't quite sure which direction this would take.

"That is perfect for you, Ryan. I'm so happy." She blinked then hugged him before rocketing off the couch and pacing. "When do you go? Soon? Do you leave soon?" She scratched her shoulder and looked around the room. "I know you said you wanted to go to school out East, so good. Will you live there? Of course, you will. How silly of me." She itched her head and laughed.

Oh, hell. She was slightly manic. "See, that's the thing…I want you to come with me." He stood, pulled her back down, and tugged on her chin, trying to capture her gaze. Her decision would either destroy his hopes and dreams or make him deliriously happy.

"Harvard is in Massachusetts." She fiddled her hands together at her waist then scratched her head again. "I-I-I live here. I live here, Ryan. In Indiana."

"We can get a place there." He kept his tone calm and nonchalant. He had to believe she'd considered their future.

"But, you are going to school there, and…and I-I am not." She gasped for breath, clutching her chest. "I'm not."

"Right." Catching her distress, he reached out and clasped her hand, rubbing the back with his thumb. "Just breathe." He squeezed her hand. "Listen, we can move away. I'll even be okay if you want your own bedroom. You could continue taking on-line classes and helping me. We've made a pretty good team this summer, don't you think?"

She stood and flopped onto the recliner, then dropped her head between her knees, fisting both hands in her hair. "I'm having trouble breathing." She looked over at him, her eyes wide. "I can't do this. I'm all itchy, and my chest hurts."

"April, look at me." He knelt beside her, tipping up her chin. "Slow breaths. In and out. In and out."

"No." She pressed both fists against her forehead, and then started banging them against her head. "No, no, no. You're leaving me. You said you wouldn't leave me."

"April, that's enough." He eased her fists to her sides before she hurt herself. "I'm taking you with me."

A shiver racked her entire body, and she shook her head. "No, Ryan, I am not ready. I'm sorry, but I can't."

"What does that mean?" His heart pounded hard, likely breaking to pieces. Now that he'd found his soul mate, he couldn't survive without her. She'd changed him, made him see that although his life had been harsh, others had survived worse. They understood each other. He'd never find that again. And the prospect of walking away from her hurt like a well-placed right hook to his chin.

Hell, did she think *he* was ready? Did she believe *he* wasn't scared over attending such a prestigious school? "Are you saying you don't want to be with me?"

"Ryan, I love you." She braced a hand on each side of his face. "I feel things inside my heart right now that I've never felt before. My stomach is flipping, and I'm worried I might vomit." She sucked in a raspy breath, and a tear trickled down her pale cheek. "All summer, I've tried to be better, tried to become a woman you would like, but I don't really know who I am yet. I've hidden away for so long, I don't have any idea what I'm doing, and the only reason I've even tried is because of you."

"I'll still help you." He pulled her closer and rested his forehead against hers.

"I'm not free." Eyes glistening, she shook her head and eased back. "I want to be April David, but I haven't figured out who she is and what she wants to do with her life. You know who you are. You're strong and brave and everything I hope to be someday." She dropped her gaze. "I am nothing."

He almost growled. "Don't do that. Don't say you're nothing. Not when you are everything. God damn you, everything." Leaning in, he kissed her lips. Softly. Reverently.

"I can't be. I'm not sure I know how to love you the right way. How can I, if I don't love myself?"

"I'll stay here until you do."

"No. No!" Her head shot back up, and she gripped his shoulders. "You will not give up this opportunity. You will go and become everything you were meant to be. I will not hold you back."

"I won't leave without you." Unable to face her doubt and resistance, he shot to his feet.

Neither spoke for a long moment. Staring out his living room window, he tried focusing on his goal, because eventually she'd agree. She had to. She said she loved him, which was everything. That was her answer...to his mind, at least.

Breaking the silence, April spoke in a quiet voice. "I tried to explain before, but perhaps, I wasn't clear enough. Do you know how hard I struggle to be here? To eat a meal prepared by someone else? I do a good job of hiding things, Ryan. I always have. But I can feel the crazy creeping back in, and with all the changes I've had this summer, I'm on the edge. Every day." She lifted her chin and met his gaze. "Sometimes my medication is the only reason I get out of bed in the morning. That, and the prospect of seeing you...and I hate it. I hate myself."

Ryan glanced over his shoulder. "Why didn't you tell me you were struggling?"

April sat on the edge of the recliner, rubbing her forehead. "I don't want you to see my broken side. I want you to see the person I'm trying to become, but if I leave with you, I will be a weight...a heavy weight, expecting too much. Asking too much. You'll be my only thing there. I won't have anything or anyone else, and you can't be my lifeline. I need to find that on my own."

"I disagree. Nothing is wrong with relying on each other.

Our whole lives have been hell, but we're together now. I *am* your lifeline, just as much as you are mine." Turning on his heel, he sank onto the coffee table and gripped her knees. "Don't let go now."

"I *am* hanging on, but too tightly."

"Fuck that, April." He shot to his feet again. "You said you loved me. Isn't that what love is about…hanging on? I need you. Please, don't say no without thinking this through."

"All right." She nodded after a tense moment. "But, can you sit, please?"

When he complied, she continued, "What am I to do while you're in class? I have no job skills. I will be of no help to you. I'm not even qualified to do basic household chores. Father has someone for all those tasks."

"We'll work it out." If housework was her only argument, he had no worries.

"You were meant for such great things." She bit her bottom lip as it trembled, and tears escaped down her cheeks. "I don't deserve anything yet, but I want to." She closed her eyes. "I want to."

"Don't." Sympathy had never worked with her. He had to harden his heart. Push. That method seemed to work. He shifted into dick-mode. "Don't you dare sit there and cry while you say you want me, love me, yet at the same time, you won't fight for us." Why couldn't she see they would continue to heal together? See they were stronger together? Maybe…just maybe, and this thought ripped out his insides, maybe she *wasn't* ready. Maybe Dewey was right all along, and he was pushing her too hard, too fast. Still…he wouldn't ease up. "You *will* think about this for a few days. I want you with me, and you'll realize it's what you want, too."

"I need to leave." After wiping her eyes, she placed her hands on the side of the chair and lifted herself out.

"Why leave? Need to get home to self-medicate?" Though he

knew the words were cruel, he couldn't stop them from coming out. His world was unraveling, and she just kept pulling the string.

"Stop it!" She shoved his chest. "You're lashing out again. Dr. Ashburn says it's—"

"Your therapist doesn't know shit about me. Plus, you've said he's holding you back. He knows if you're cured he won't get any more of that David cash." He almost laughed at that, because wasn't *he* one to talk. He'd made a mess of things, but his heart hurt. "You will stay here, and we'll finish discussing this. No more running off to hide. You escaped, remember?" He pressed a finger against her left shoulder. "No longer a caged bird, April. Don't go back."

April flicked a hand across her cheek, wiping away her tears. "You're not being fair. You expect me to just upend my life without thinking everything through. I do love you. I do. But right now, you're hurting me." She took two steps toward the door then stopped and hung her head. "I wish I could be like the heroine in a novel and just sweep from the room. Leave you behind so you couldn't see my pain, but I can't drive, Ryan. I can't walk down the street without being accosted by photographers, so I'll ask again, please, take me home."

He studied her wilted form for a moment then cursed and grabbed his cell and keys off the kitchen counter. He brushed by her on his way out the door then turned back and grabbed her arm. "I can't stand it. Don't go home and take the drugs, April. Don't do it. You're strong enough on your own."

"I hurt." She lifted a hand to her breastbone.

"So do I."

"I'm afraid. Losing you will send me someplace I've never been. I've lived in the darkness for so long, but without you it'll be worse. I just know it."

"Damn it, April." He shook her arm. "I never said you would lose me."

She met his gaze before placing her open palm against his

cheek. "I want you to go away, and while you're gone, I'll work on being better."

He kissed her hand, feeling defeated though he couldn't say why. Maybe because he wasn't enough for her to change. For her to move past her demons, and he wanted to be. And that shit hurt. A foreign hurt. Why couldn't she just be his April? Why did she have to let the past control her life, and in doing so, control his? "You're fine now."

"No, Ryan." She shook her head. "I'm really not."

"I'll take you home, but I want you to consider coming with me, and I don't want you to take any drugs." He paused with his hand on the door handle and spoke the words he'd never said to anyone. "I love you. I'm seriously pissed at you right now, but I still love you."

She tugged on his shoulder and spun him around. "You love me?"

He met her gaze. "Yeah, I do."

"Will you kiss me then?"

Unable to fight the plea in her eyes, he bent and did just that. He owned her mouth, kissing her like a man fighting for his last breath, and in essence, he was. Minutes passed, maybe hours, but he kept her in his arms, showing her that he did, in fact, love her. "See what we create together, the passion between us? I won't let you go without a fight. I've never loved anyone until you."

"Ryan, please consider who I really am. I am not this fantasy female you've made me out to be. I'm not a heroine. I'm so very far from normal."

"So am I." He shrugged.

"Sometimes, when you hold me, I get claustrophobic and can barely contain this inner scream to break free. I hate the feeling. I wish it away, but it still happens." She huffed out a laugh. "When you went to the bathroom earlier, I washed off my salad. Three times, because it was one of those bagged salads, and people get sick from those." She bit her bottom lip and sighed. "I didn't want to do it, but I couldn't stop. I don't want you to see *that* April, the crazy girl who takes over sometimes. I need to get rid of her, and then I can give you everything."

"I'll take her." He held her tight. "She doesn't scare me. I'll even buy the bitch a salad spinner."

With a soft laugh, April leaned up and lightly kissed his lips.

A kiss that felt too much like goodbye.

"Take me home, please."

Realizing round one was over, he agreed and walked her home. After watching her walk into the townhouse with drooped shoulders, he realized he should dig a little deeper into her issues. Read about PTSD. Perhaps talk to Dr. Ashburn. Ryan wasn't afraid of her phobias, but did he really understand that part of her personality? He'd been wrapped up in everything *he* wanted and hadn't asked about her progress. As friends, he'd figured she'd tell him her troubles, but she'd been alone for so long and he shouldn't expect three months to change all that.

He needed to know more about who she was before she'd met him. Maybe they did need time to know each other better. Still, they'd both come so far. He wouldn't give up now.

CHAPTER 18

After leaving April alone for the weekend, Ryan considered his next plan of action. He needed more information in order to win this case—the most important case of his life. He'd called the senator and asked to meet with him Monday morning. Unknown pieces of April's life still existed, and he hoped her father could shed a little light.

After ringing the townhouse's doorbell, he was led inside by the housekeeper. At the door of the senator's study, he knocked then stepped inside.

David was on the phone, but he indicated with a jerk of his head that Ryan could enter then he waved a hand toward the coffee machine.

After dropping in a French Roast pod, Ryan studied the pictures lined up on a bookshelf. Some were of politicians, some of local celebrities, others he had no clue, but then from a higher shelf, he pulled down a picture of the senator with two blondes— a likely five-year-old April, standing beside his wife. Anna had her hands on April's shoulders. They all smiled, the perfect blonde family. April did look like her mother, only a softer version. He brushed his finger against the frame, dust formed on his finger. This little girl had no idea the trials awaiting her.

He cleared his throat to remove the solid lump of pity and

sadness that threatened to choke him. What if his child went through April's horrors? *Whoa!* His head was all over the place. He'd never even considered having kids. Why was he even thinking such a thing? He shook his head and picked up his steaming coffee.

Ryan set the photo back on the shelf but noted a few more of Anna and April. He plucked one of April taken maybe a few years ago, sitting at a table in a library. A professional photo, which evoked a lot of questions. Had she left her safe haven to get this photo taken, or was a library located in this townhouse? Her gaze seemed vacant, and she was so very thin. Too thin. The girl needed more protein.

"Mr. Cole, what brings you in on this steamy August Monday?"

"Just that." Ryan turned and lumbered over to his regular seat in front of the senator's desk. "It's late August, and I'm heading East soon. I spoke to April about coming with me, and she doesn't feel she's ready."

"She did seem rather quiet at breakfast yesterday."

Ryan placed his coffee cup on a glass side table. "I don't know enough about her past. She's worried about some of her...phobias. And now that she's brought them up, I'm worried, too. I've never dealt with...well, with persons suffering from mental problems. The thing is, I think she's normal enough, so either I just don't see them or I'm missing something."

"Did you expect her to be cured after three months?" The senator steepled his fingers under his chin.

"Cured of what, exactly? She talks about this therapist all the time. You need to check into that guy. Not sure he's helping."

"I disagree." The senator smiled and shook his head. "Dr. Ashburn spoke to me just this morning. Apparently, April had called, asking to meet with him today."

"Great." She hadn't come to *him*. That didn't bode well for their future. Not at all.

"You want to know about April's issues, well one of them is her constant need to discuss her problems with her therapist."

"What about the meds?"

The senator scratched his chin. "I believe she's moved off a few. Although, some she may need her whole life."

Ryan rubbed his temple and took a drink of his lukewarm coffee. "What can I do to convince her she'll be fine with me in Cambridge?"

"I don't know that you can." David tapped his fingers against his desk. "Why can't you give her some time to adjust to the idea?"

His knee bopped up and down again. *Damn it.* "I'm selfish. I want her with me."

"I understand, but *you* must understand that your wishes might not be what's best for her." Shoving aside his laptop, the senator leaned forward, placing his elbows on his paper-covered desk. "I am pleased you've grown to care for my daughter. I knew you'd be a good match, and you *have* brought her out of her shell, *but*"—he raised a finger—"she's been hidden away for a long time. She shouldn't be forced to make rash and emotionally-driven decisions."

"I love her." Why couldn't that be enough? *Because, dumbass, maybe in loving her, and accepting who she is, I should allow her to heal at her own pace.* That thought sucked. Why must he possess an argumentative internal filter?

"You love her *now*." The senator sat back. "What happens when you get in with the college crowd? You'll make new friends. Meet new women."

"April is the only person who knows me." Having her father suggest he couldn't be faithful, irritated his already frayed nerves.

"Don't have to know a woman to be with her. One-night stands were more your thing, weren't they?"

"*Were* being the operative word, *sir.*" Ryan would love nothing more than to wipe that all-knowing smirk off the senator's face, but April's father was only revealing the truth. And Ryan *had* come to bring everything out in the open. "Do you think April could handle this move?"

The senator tapped a pen against his desk. "Maybe, in time. And maybe you need time, as well. I forced this relationship on you for my own purposes. Perhaps you need time away to clear your head."

"My head is very clear. I know what I want."

A door shut somewhere upstairs.

The senator's phone buzzed on his desk, but after glancing at the screen, he ignored the call. "Cole, I appreciate what you did for me months ago, and I appreciate what you've done for my daughter this summer. Because I've come to respect you, I'll continue to back your relationship with April as much as I'm able. Paying for your education seems a small sacrifice for you befriending April. You've done exactly as I've hired you to do."

"I'm telling her the truth." Ryan kept the senator's gaze, daring him to disagree. "Maybe not for a few years, but I won't keep this from her forever."

"No need, Ryan. *She* already knows." April's sweet voice reverberated through her father's office, stopping his heart cold.

CHAPTER 19

After swallowing his pride and begging her to hear their explanation, Ryan settled April into his chair in her father's office. He stood at her side, holding her hand.

During the complete retelling of their scheme, she remained quiet, but once her father finished, she met Ryan's gaze. "So, you never really worked at the teashop?"

He would explain and they would move on. He had to believe that. "No." *Great start, Cole.* "I mean, I did work there, but I actually worked for your father."

"That seems strange." Her brow furrowed. "Did Mr. Jones know?"

"Yes, April," her father replied. "I own the building, and we came to an agreement, of sorts."

"I see. So, once again you used your money and influence to try and fix poor, broken April."

"April." Ryan squeezed her hand and used a stern tone. "That isn't fair. He was trying to help you."

"By paying people to be my friend? How is that supposed to make me feel? I told you I wanted to stand on my own." She glared at Ryan then faced her father. "I told *you,* as well. And yet, here we are. Or, actually, I don't know where I am or how I feel about all this, except disappointed."

"You can be mad all you want, but your father's plan *did* work. We *are* right for each other, so why does it matter how we came together?"

"Because your scheme makes me doubt myself. Makes me think I can't make friends on my own. How do you even know you like me? You're dazzled by dollar signs."

"I'll take that." Ryan pressed his lips together and nodded. "I deserve your anger right now."

"What about what I deserve?" She ripped away her hand. "Why should I be lied to? Why should I let you two lead me around like a puppet on a string? You've made me believe I was dancing on my own when all along *you* controlled the music."

"April, calm down." Her father lifted a hand. "I realize you're—"

"Stop it! Don't you dare take that tone with me." She shot out of her chair. "I'm late for an appointment, and I don't want to hear any more, anyway. I might be a while, as I'll likely spend the rest of the day explaining to the therapist this...this...idiotic plan you two contrived." April stomped her foot. "I'm furious with you both."

Wow. Defiant April apparently did it for him, but those thoughts were inappropriate when he was standing on a sinking ship. "Is Dewey going with you?"

"No."

"Then I'll take you."

"I can go by myself," she practically screamed.

"April Anna David that is enough." The senator rose to his feet. "Ryan is right. You will not go out alone in your current state. I'll alert Dewey."

"No. I will call him. I've had enough of you doing *things* for me." She folded both arms across her chest. "And, one more *thing*...even though I wasn't invited to your little plan-April's-life meeting, I will say, when someone does a good job, you pay them. Ryan did a good job, so you will follow through on whatever you agreed. Do you understand me, Father?"

David came around his desk and stood before her. "April, I'm sorry."

"For what? For buying a friendship? For lying about who I am? Yes, I suppose I'm still a little bitter about that." She sniffed. "I know I haven't been an easy child to raise. I understand why you resorted to such measures, but next time...next time, maybe just ask me. Talk to me. I've needed your guidance all along, and I'm sorry, but this wasn't the right way to lead me." She huffed out a laugh. "But...well, it worked, didn't it? You should be happy, I guess. Ryan did help me. Your *employee* did his job."

This conversation was starting to take a very bad turn. "April, damn it." Ryan braced both hands on his hips. "I am not his employee...okay, so, maybe yes... he's paying me...but...I'm not his employee. Everything you've heard today changes nothing. I still need you. I want you to come with me. That will never change."

April swallowed visibly then straightened her shoulders. "I know that in my head but not in my heart. I need to be away from you two for a while. My life is upside down enough. I just want to be April. No one else, and I'm so close, but this revelation just might set me back a few steps." She heaved a deep breath and faced her father. "Finalize your business with Ryan, he deserves everything."

That said, she padded out but didn't slam the door. The woman needed to learn the proper way to throw a fit.

Heart aching, he followed her out into the hall. "April, we can work this out." He gripped her arm and spun her around to face him. Desperation nipped at his heels, driving him almost to violence. She couldn't do this, couldn't leave him until they'd talked this through. "Stay here and we'll talk."

"I don't want to." She kept her gaze on the floor, her voice soft. "Not right now. You see me as this weak creature you need to save. I won't fit into this mold you've already set for me, or the mold my father wants. I can only be me. I thought I was finding her, but now…" She shrugged. "Now, I'd like some time."

"How much time?"

"I don't know." She started toward the stairs that led to her room.

"April, stop." He kept his hold on her arm. "I won't have you escaping to your room so you can question everything that's happened. Only one thing matters: I love you. Your father did pay me to be your friend. But no one could pay me to love you."

"All right, Ryan. You've said your piece." She glanced toward the stairs. "I need some quiet time. Please, just go."

A fracture started at the top of his heart, threatening to splinter him apart. If she wasn't holding him together, then nothing but rage and pain would exist. "We are supposed to stand strong together. Don't break now. Please, April."

Her stance said, don't touch. Her eyes cold. And the stillness was almost more than he could bear. The quiet. The not knowing. He never should have lied to her, but then he'd never of known her. He didn't know which was worse.

After a moment, April squeezed his hand on her arm. "Let me go. I can't stand with you if I can't stand alone. And right now, I'm falling apart. Please, just give me some time. I love you, so I will forgive you, but I don't know what to do after that."

"Then let me guide you." He kissed her then, trying desperately to break down the barrier she'd begun to build between them. "Don't do this. I'm so sorry. I never meant to hurt you. Ever." He kissed her cheek and the tip of her nose.

Easing away, she pressed her forehead against his chest. "I've been led around for too long. My father, and now you. I need to stand on my own and distinguish what is real and what isn't."

"This is real." He kissed her again. Hard. With every ounce of hope he had left in his frightened, shattering heart. He couldn't lose her, not now. "I made a mistake that wasn't really a mistake, because I have you. I wouldn't change anything."

"I've always been in such awe of you." She caressed his cheek. "I just wish, for once, you were in awe of me." With a sad smile, she slipped out of his arms and headed up the stairs.

# # #

Days passed, and April always said the same thing when he called or texted. She loved him but needed to discover herself without any help from the men in her life.

The time came to pack up and move to Harvard, and losing the battle, he left her behind. But he kept hope in his heart that someday she'd understand he loved every part of her broken, different, beautiful self. Each and every piece.

Over the summer, they had become a team, and in every way, they belonged together. They had aligned and sealed all the empty places deep within each other. All the past pain eased by a mutual understanding and forever love.

So, he'd wait.

And wait he did...for three long years.

EPILOGUE

Fucking tie was choking him.

Working his way to the bar, Ryan nodded greetings and stopped to chitchat with those who congratulated him—professors and alumni.

He stopped at the bar, ordered a rum and Coke, and was joined by Dick York, senior partner and the head of the Family Law division at York and Graff.

"Ready for Maine, son?" York slapped him on the back.

"Absolutely, sir."

More people joined them, and he listened with half an ear, until a familiar male voice broke through the din.

Senator David had entered the room.

Ryan's heart thundered. Was April with him? He sidestepped to glance around Dick York's robust form but could only see, Cheri.

Still...*she* was here. He could sense her. Feel her. His entire body electrified. He excused himself and made his way to the senator.

Then she walked in.

Everything stopped like a movie reel pausing before switching to slo-mo.

Stunning. Absolutely breathtaking. Her blonde hair was bound high in some elaborate twist. A tight, navy-blue and white dress that accentuated every one of her curves, and she wore a lethal smile meant only for him.

He wanted to throw her down right here, right now. Claim her, own her. How dare she appear out of nowhere looking like a million bucks on five-inch heels?

He watched as she inhaled deeply just prior to stopping two steps before him, though she wobbled a little in those heels. Good, she was just as off kilter as him.

"Hello, Ryan."

Thank you for reading *For April*. I hope you enjoyed Ryan and April's story. If you did, <u>please leave a review at your purchase site</u>. Reviews are very appreciated by the author. I'm "moose"-assuredly grateful.

Visit www.jillianjacobs.com
for all new release information.

Please enjoy the following excerpt from *Ember's Center*, Book #1 in The O-Line Series. Jillian's Contemporary with Suspenseful Elements.

Owen smiled when she finally met his melted-chocolate eyes.

Seemingly aware she'd given him an once-over—a very blatant once-over. *Awkward.* She clasped together her trembling hands. "Was there something you needed?"

"Yes, actually."

His voice matched his body: deep and heavy, and she bit back a sigh.

"I have a small problem you might help me with."

"Absolutely. What is it?" Ember folded both arms across her chest. *Where are my shoes? Can he see the tea stain on my shirt?*

"I'm glad you agree. You see, I hate when women cry."

What? That was quite the non-sequitur. Laugh lines appeared beside his eyes. Unsure what her answer should be, she replied, "I hate when women cry, too."

Not comfortable around men, especially huge, handsome ones with square jaws sharp enough to cut ice, Ember calmed her breathing and tried stilling her pounding heart. The Marauders' center stood in her cube entry.

Her entry. *Oh no! Where has my mind strayed?*

Did he live up to the rumors? The "O" in Offensive-line raised many a woman's curiosity across social and traditional media platforms since all the players were extraordinarily gorgeous. Not hard to imagine Owen's reputation for bedroom proclivity was very accurate since his shoes were so big, which meant he was big everywhere. *Ridiculous.* She would not stare *there.*

Maintain eye contact. Keep it!

About the Author

In the spring of 2013, Jillian Jacobs changed her career path and became a romance writer. After reading for years, she figured writing a romance would be quick and easy. Nope! With the guidance of the Indiana Romance Writers of America (IRWA) chapter, she's learned many "rules" to writing a proper romance. Being re-schooled was an interesting journey, and she hopes the best trails are yet to be traveled.

Water's Threshold, the first in Jillian's Elementals series, was a finalist in Chicago-North's 2014 Fire and Ice contest in the Women's Fiction category.

Jillian's volunteer efforts include:

- IRWA 2014 and 2015 Program Chair
- IRWA 2015 and 2017 Conference Co-chair
- On The Far Side coordinator for the 2015 and 2016 Fantasy, Futuristic, and Paranormal chapter.

She is the co-founder of Healing with Words—a not for profit agency established for healing survivors of abuse, addiction, trafficking, and prostitution. The mission is to bring together readers, authors, and survivors in a positive manner that affects change and relief from negative influences. Writers on The River, an author event in Peoria, Illinois is hosted by Healing With Words.

Her genres are Paranormal and Contemporary with suspenseful

Connect with Jillian Jacobs:

Website: www.jillianjacobs.com
Twitter: https://twitter.com/GreenMooseProd
Facebook: https://www.facebook.com/GreenMooseProd/
Amazon Author Page: http://bit.ly/JillianJacobsAMZAuthorPage
Goodreads: https://www.goodreads.com/JillianJacobs
Newsletter:
https://landing.mailerlite.com/webforms/landing/q2h3g1